Born to Die

Lezleigh Vincent

Publisher's note: *Born To Die* is the work of the author's imagination.
Resemblance to actual events / persons is purely coincidental or
smeared with Lezleigh's imagination.

Printed in the United States of America
Edited, formatted, and interior design by Kristen Corrects, Inc.
Cover art design by Daria Volyanskaya

First edition published 2016
10 9 8 7 6 5 4 3 2 1

Vincent, Lezleigh
Born to die / Lezleigh Vincent
p. cm.
ASIN: B01GNHLTCQ
ISBN-13: 978-1533580344
ISBN-10: 1533580340

For Mark:
For teaching a gypsy soul the art of equanimity. For recognizing that my fullest expression would only be achieved once set free. That, my friend, is love. I'm quite certain that if you tried, you could walk on water.

Table of Contents

Preface
1901

I am on the shower floor looking into my dilated eyes with a compact mirror. I took my last shower like a warrior going into battle—just the way he showed me. The circumstances were off again. I'm still caught in the loop. There's a reason I checked into this inn.

I struggle to my feet and open the windows. Engulfed by the gust of the scent from the magnolias, my damp hair tousles as I turn to see the bed we shared. Room number 323. It had to be this exact room and June 20. An esoteric message only he would understand.

I didn't want to do it at home. I didn't want my son to find me and live the rest of his life with the image of his mother dead on the floor.

Exhaustion is here now, enveloping me with her weary ways. I put on *the* nightgown. I get in *the* bed. It smells different without him. A pang to the gut. The wreckage begins to fall as droplets of memories. A child's laughter comes from the street as if this were any ordinary day. The draft blows a picture off the wall. It lands on the floor beside the bed. As I look down, I am stunned by the content. Time won't stop. Circumstances will not change.

I remember asking Brahma, Allah, Jah, Olodumare, Christ, Jehovah, El-Olam, God, the Collective for the visceral human experience. I asked for the tactile embodiment of flesh. Part of me wanted to stay there raptured in spirit—but the desire to touch him, to taste him, to hear him, to breathe with him once more was too powerful.

Tears leak out the slits of my eyes and drop into my ears. I open my mouth and shiver at the cold metallic taste on my lips. Serenity rides on the next breeze. I welcome her to my

Lezleigh Vincent

asylum. Why aim for the roof of my mouth? Why risk being both faceless *and* soulless? The barrel on my tongue, my thumb on the trigger, I aim through my mouth straight for the back of my head. I squeeze and blow my own brains into the pillow. My blood splatters onto the painted canvas of butterflies and sunflowers below.

Prologue: Butterflies
1937

I don't remember the first time I contemplated suicide. The compound prescription beckoned my gaze a little longer. How much powder would it take to eliminate my petite frame? Maybe stepping onto the train tracks or a quick gunshot to the temple. I flirted with the idea of self-inflicted death. I was secretly envious of the dead. They defied the emptiness that permeates the soul when you live without the person you love the most.

What is it called when two people exchange meaningful dialogue across a crowded room without uttering words? What makes a couple nostalgic even before the moment is gone? Pheromones? Momentary infatuation? Is that a soulmate connection? A twin flame? Eros? Does passion have an expiration date? What is the shelf life of desire? Is it possible to maintain stability, ease, familiarity, consistency, comfort, adventure, excitement, newness...even butterflies?

Butterflies. Please allow me to qualify the word as I once experienced it. The butterflies I felt contained the g-force of a fighter jet. Their magnitude possessed the energy of a powerful quake within the earth of my soul. They were the churning of a powerful desire at my epicenter. The word *butterflies* conjures up a soft image, but if you have ever experienced their excruciatingly delightful ways, you know them to be an elusive phenomenon that evokes feelings paramount to anything you've ever experienced.

To know the ecstasy of butterflies—but to live without them—had become unbearable for me. I was a shell of myself. Everything looked the same on the outside, but the void within pervaded like a cancerous infection. My dissonance grew until my decay was imminent. Because of my decision to do the right thing, I was dying a slow, torturous death. Amelia Earhart recently said: "Being alone is scary but not as scary as being alone in a relationship." I am so lonely.

He did not help my demise, but he was also decomposing. My decision was killing him. He conspired with the Universe to signal his grief. He would deliver an esoteric method of torture. It would be a sign only I could comprehend. Maybe I would find a butterfly trapped in a glass jar or a loose bouquet of sunflowers held by strands of my long copper hair. He found ways to demonstrate his distress. My avatar was calling me to a divide.

According to Greek mythology, soulmates are two people who come together because of similarities, love, and friendship. Soulmates are plentiful. Twin flames are very different. Twin flames are made of the same soul—split into two. They reincarnate over many lifetimes and have an unprecedented longing for each other. A rare energy flows between them distinguishable by vibration, intensity, and clarity of desire. When they recognize each other, there is an unspoken understanding: they feel unified. Yet the intensity of this connection can cause one flame to be the "runner."

That's what I did last time—I ran. Now, I was tired of running away from my feelings. I was exhausted from stuffing my longings down into the darkest part of my bowels where things rot. Withholding myself from him was paralyzing. I was a helicopter in a downward spiral, sputtering out of control.

So the shift finally happened. I went outside in my nightgown and started to run. My gait strengthened despite my bare feet slapping the pavement. My stride reached a steady cadence in the center of the street. *Hit me*, I dared anyone driving in a car. *Hit me! And if you're going to hit me, then take me out!*

With tears cascading, I ran in the direction of the inn. Was I really going to do this? Was I really going to choose my own happiness? Choosing me meant choosing him. My passion. My mirror. My twin flame. I was tired of denying myself the pleasure of his love. Even I had underestimated the power of my feelings. Clarity set in. My resolve took me by surprise and fueled my determination. He is the *one*. The urgency besieged me like a tsunami. When I was hurt, he woke up to pain. When he was sad, I was fatigued. We reflected the lightest and even the darkest of each other's image.

This epiphany penetrated me to my core. I had never felt anything more visceral. It carried me through the streets toward the inn. Each stride felt closer to freedom. Light was collecting around the door to my captivity. The cage was opening.

Morning was considering its ascent, but dark clung like a heavy cloak. Rain pelted against my back. Thunder clapped as loudly as my heart. I shouted to him telepathically, wondering if he could actually feel me awakening to what he already knew. He could always feel my emotions, sometimes before me. I knew he could feel them now. *It's a boy!* I wanted to shout to the world. My clairvoyant proclamation was waking him out of a deep slumber.

My arms pumped; my breath was a cloud in the air. The ground was a treadmill. My legs couldn't carry me there fast enough. I imagined his strong square jaw, his thick dark hair, his rich brown eyes. I pictured his handsome face glowing when I finally say the words he had been longing to hear. *Don't go! I choose us.*

Arriving at this junction, I had to make a decision. Stay the path or diverge. I had finally arrived at the intersection of *Fuck It* and *I Don't Care*. We had sacrificed our souls' true desires long enough. For once in my adult life I was going to choose *me*. My happiness. I was going to be selfish.

My heart thrashed from my sprint. My gown billowed as I ran. Rounding the corner of the magnolia tree-lined street, I ran to the inn.

The headlights flashed behind me. At first I thought it was lightning. Then I heard the engine roar. The tires splashed through the water. I felt the rain spatter my back before the impact.

I didn't feel pain but my vantage point immediately changed. I was floating, looking down at my body through the branches of a magnolia tree. My body lay still, mangled on the asphalt. My ribs were twisted and snapped like a twig used for kindling. The ribs he called a perfect triangle—his fingers had memorized the divots between each groove. The sternum he placed his hand against, eyes closed, to feel our hearts' connection. The hipbones that landed exactly under his. My hand still cradled my abdomen in a futile effort to shield our creation.

He heard the explosive thud and charged from the inn. Up high through the branches, I watched him run to me. He knew what I was coming to say, he felt it. He had that disoriented morning look, his hair pressed firmly against his scalp. His sprint halted a few feet from my body. His face was contorted in a ghastly expression. He let out a shriek that raptured night and penetrated dawn.

His hands smacked hard against his mouth. He approached me the way one would teeter on a tightrope. Slowly and cautiously he swayed, struggling to keep his balance. He collapsed to his knees so hard it drew blood. As if worshiping an idol, he knelt beside me. I could only see his hair as he looked down at my body. I had memorized the back of his neck long ago when I woke up encasing him. He was a quiet sleeper, only making noises when he wanted more of me. He gasped and clawed his face "Oh God!" he yelled in a throaty cry I had never heard.

He thrust his head back and bellowed in agony. He looked right through me into the sky. "Why? Why take her away from me now? She finally recognized me! This was supposed to be our chance. She was my twin…you promised. Why now, God? Why?" He sucked in air with a popping sound. He slowly brought his gaze back to my body on the ground. In the same tenderness of a father to a child, he placed his hand under my neck, lifting my head. My bones crunched in his palm. He flinched, blowing mucus out of his nose. He leaned over me and lowered his face. His mouth covered mine. His will to breathe life back into my body shot out of him like rockets of desire.

Looking down at my body on the ground, I saw my blood-soaked garment was tattered and shredded away from my skin, exposing my navel. His head tilted back as he wept. A tear rolled down his cheek, onto his chin, and dropped into the center of my belly button. It was his DNA.

I zoomed in, tightening on my view of my stomach. Something was moving. A caterpillar began to wriggle and slither out of my navel. My body was simply a cocoon. The bug slowly inched, twisting its way out of my belly. In moments it metamorphosed into a radiant butterfly.

Suddenly there was a swarm of butterflies. They fluttered up and around the branches that encircled me. The butterflies lit up like vibrant fireflies and surrounded me floating in the tree. They emitted thousands of hues of yellow, slowly making the shape of a sunflower. They discharged a euphoric serum into my body. At first I thought it was the wind, but it was the whisper of the butterflies delivering a sound through their light.

Time and space never hinder communication between souls who connect by the heart. It is time to come home. Rest now. He is your twin flame. You will recognize him again next time.

I slowly lost focus, my lids covered my eyes, and the butterflies carried me away.

1

"It's too late to get away from it all
I'm done with running so I give it to you."
– Nirvana

The council gathers; she has come forth with great desire. This is her last incarnation.

As if packing a bag, we bring in her warrior spirit. On final incarnations, humans must procreate; therefore, her twin flame will be a male. Of course, she will have free will. If her craving is strong, she will trigger recollections of déjà vu. We prepare the recipe that makes up her genes. The ingredients will result in a human woman.

They will call her Macy Oona Rivers.

We have an abundance of love for you humans. Although you make many of your decisions based on misconceived teachings and flawed historical accounts, we adore you collectively and individually just the same.

For centuries, people have contemplated the existence of God. The word *God* makes us sound like a single entity. Many envision us as a man with a long gray beard up on a cloud. But we are simply conscious energy from the very source that created you. We vibrate love. We are many, aligned into one council of Collective Consciousness. We are Oona; oneness.

The incarnation begins. We increase our vibration. Faint light grows in size, vibrating a modestly audible sound. Our light becomes a blazing glitter; the sound crescendos. We stir up, swirl, emit luminous fragments. Our molecules dance. Robust energy spills out, twisting into a vigorous shimmering cylindrical prism. We circulate into a vortex.

At the pinnacle of our orgasmic delight, we explode. We burst and scatter in feather-like thin particles. The gentle breeze carries us like a dandelion's pappus. The council has agreed.

It is done.

First breath.

2

"Hey pretty girl, won't you look my way?
Love's in the air tonight
You can bet you make this old boy's day
Hey pretty girl, won't you look my way?"
— *Kip Moore*

In October 1997, Macy awakened to the warm sun spilling through the window. The smell of fresh paint was less potent. Thumbtacks held an old sheet over the bright window. Daniel had asked her to get blinds. She would do that today, she decided.

Boxes marked *dishes* and *shoes* filled the new house. The only picture on the wall was of their wedding kiss on a gorgeous March day. She could hear the squeak from the closet. *It's his sock against the shoehorn guiding his foot into the brown leather shoe. Only my husband would use one of those.* The thought made her giggle as she rolled over and stretched.

"Husband," she whispered in a hushed voice. The word still sounded fresh on her tongue. People said they were a balanced yin and yang. Macy Oona Westcott. Macy Westcott. Westcott. She was still getting used to the sound. She took a deep breath and exhaled with an audible catcall. She threw her arms over her head and stretched long.

Hearing her high-pitched screech, Daniel poked his head around the closet and laughed. "Good morning Kitty Cat, did I wake you up?"

"Nah," she answered as she pretended to snore. He playfully dashed from the closet, change clinging in his pocket, as he pounced on her, straddling her on the bed. He pinned her hands down and pressed his fresh minty mouth on hers.

"Ugh, No, don't!" She laughed. "I have terrible morning breath. I can taste it." With a swift movement, she somersaulted over him.

"Hi," she huffed in his face with an exaggerated "H" and blew her breath in his direction.

"Eww...garlic!" he teased and pretended to faint.

The sheet stayed tucked into the mattress, exposing her breasts to his face. He took a deep breath, lifted his head to the center of her chest, and exhaled loudly, making an abrupt clapping noise to her skin.

"Motorboat!" they both exclaimed together as she shimmied her shoulders back and forth, shaking her bare breasts in his face. Their spirited morning rendezvous continued until he realized his shoe was touching the bedspread.

"I gotta get to the office. I don't want to make a bad first impression."

She smiled warmly at him. "You couldn't do that if you tried. They're going to love you."

He appreciated her positive nature. She was always affirming things. It was the yogi in her.

"What's your schedule today?" he asked.

"Tumbling 10:00 to 1:00 then to the Metta Yoga Studio to teach a 2:00 vinyasa, 4:00 yin, and 5:00 kundalini."

"God bless you," he joked about the Sanskrit word as he gently nudged her off him. She rolled over with ease and fell back into the pillows. "Try to go back to sleep," he encouraged with a whisper. "You'll be up late at your gig tonight."

At 6:45 AM the sun was beginning to reveal itself. Macy's hair was a long, copper undulating wave that sprawled the length of the pillow. *How did it fall perfectly like that?* he wondered. He was glad she had agreed to soften her untamed mane. He could run his fingers all the way from scalp to the ends now. He appreciated that she didn't care what other people thought when she wore her hair in dreadlocks, but they were living in a more conservative area and they were getting older.

"What?" she asked. He was staring at her.

"Nothing. You're just beautiful." He ran his hands through her hair. He stood and stiffly smoothed over his shirt several times as he looked at his reflection in the mirror. He glanced at her, eagerly waiting for praise.

"Well, you're a sexy employed video gamer!" she teased. "You look great. Don't forget your pager. Good luck!" She ruffled his shirt and pulled him down for one more kiss. "Just do that thing you do when you're being you and they'll love you." She winked at her tongue twister. Moments later she heard the garage door open and close.

Macy and Daniel had moved from San Diego and settled into an eclectic neighborhood in Raleigh, North Carolina. Mr. and Mrs. Westcott lived two hours away in Wilmington in Daniel's childhood home. A year before, Macy's parents, Oona and Carl Rivers, moved forty-five minutes from Raleigh to Rolesville, North Carolina. Now that both sets of parents were in North Carolina, Macy and Daniel decided it was time to move. They were ready to make a family. The cost of living on the West Coast was astronomical. Daniel was always fond of North Carolina and Macy was usually up for an adventure.

Homes in Raleigh were well appointed with granite countertops, stainless steel appliances, and sizable yards. Macy could not believe they were homeowners. They could have never afforded a three-bedroom home on the West Coast. Daniel used the spare bedroom as an office. Each subdivision boasted a swimming pool. Every housewife belonged to a gym or yoga studio.

Before they moved, Daniel scouted out the areas. He was excited about his new job as a software developer for a graphic design firm that developed video games. It was a nice change to be in North Carolina, though he had forgotten about the humidity. The traffic was nothing to speak of comparatively. Their neighborhood was in the Five Points area, close to downtown Raleigh. Daniel enjoyed being near his alma mater. He caught up with old friends quickly at Hayes Barton, the old soda shop turned posh café. He was glad to be back.

For their wedding, Mrs. Westcott arranged for Macy and Daniel to get married in a small chapel in their exclusive neighborhood. The Kenan Chapel was lovely, but Macy preferred to get married in a rustic barn near an open pasture. Mrs. Westcott did not approve and insisted on the country club at Landfall. Many of the Westcotts' friends would be invited and it wouldn't be sufficient to have the wedding in a barn. Carl walked Macy down the aisle and Oona ended up being her only bridesmaid. Daniel's dad was his best man even though the two barely spoke since Daniel's freshman year in college. Carl was presented the bill for use of the country club and was happy to give his only daughter a beautiful wedding. He made sure food and drinks flowed with an open bar and the seven-piece band kept the guests dancing into the morning.

Macy worried that her father had spent his retirement savings on this one day. Carl generously dismissed his daughter's concerns: "You only get married once," he'd said. Daniel and Macy still enjoyed flooding over their wedding album. Macy's favorite picture was taken at their reception. She had taken off her shoes to dance. Daniel lifted her up so her feet were standing on top of his shoes. He held her tight and lifted one leg at a time so they could dance in sync. More pictures would be hung in the dining room once the couple settled into their house.

Macy had been married to Daniel long enough to know hanging a picture on the wall was an intricate process. He would use the ruler and tape measure, precisely marking the walls. Then he would calculate the area and perimeter of the frame to the length of the wall. It was the engineer in him. Back in her single days, Macy hung artwork with one slam of her hiking boot. She grew her own lettuce and made her own almond milk. She avoided things that needed to be dry-cleaned. If she couldn't use her homemade detergent and hand wash the garment on her grandmother's old washing board, she wouldn't buy it.

Macy got out of her new bed, stretched, and strolled to the en-suite bathroom. She leaned into the mirror for a moment and saw the girl in front of her becoming a woman. So much had changed since she got married. Her hair was soft and wavy now compared to when they met. They owned their house.

She sat tall on the toilet seat and peered out the window. A neighbor about to begin his morning commute. Kids on the street waiting for the bus. Someone's mother waiting with the group. The lady held a cup of coffee in one hand and a leash to her dog on the other. She wasn't that much older than Macy. *Maybe I'll be standing at the bus stop with a kid someday.* She wiped, flushed, washed her hands and face.

As Macy brushed her teeth, she looked closely at the woman with foamed teeth gazing back at her in the mirror. She contracted her abdominals and turned to the side. In addition to yoga, she ran several days a week and led gymnastics classes for seven- and eight-year-olds. She was pleased with her physique. She had not smoked pot in over two years. Daniel had been a positive influence.

She rinsed her mouth and leaned in closer to the mirror. She noticed a few lighter hairs escaping from her temples. She fluffed her hair to cover them and went back into the bedroom.

Macy padded over to a wooden trunk in the corner of their new room. She lifted the lid with effort. Shortly before she met Daniel, she lived in Pune, India for two months. She was given the opportunity to learn from one of the most respected yoga teachers in the world. The trunk was one of her keepsakes from that pivotal time. Bellur Krashnamachar Sundararaja Lyengar changed her life forever during that trip. Macy came back to the States invigorated, alive, at peace, and one with the universe.

Re-entry into American society was baffling. She spent her first day back in the US in silent meditation. Nothing had changed while she was away. All that changed was Macy.

The trunk squeaked loudly when Macy opened it. She reached in for the tapestry. Her eyes closed as she felt around for it. Her tongue came to the crease of her mouth. She bit down slightly in deep concentration.

She knew the fabric as soon as her fingers touched it, as she'd spent many days memorizing the threads with her fingertips. The stitches were woven together to create a beautiful pattern that bore a design of a tiny elephant with a sunflower behind its ear and a huge butterfly sitting on its trunk. Macy had passed it several times in the street markets. One day, she saw it—really saw it for the first time. She grabbed it with haste. She couldn't believe that she had passed it so many times without actually seeing it. She negotiated with the vendor and made the purchase.

Daniel thought the tapestry was tacky and smelled odd, so it only made appearances during Macy's meditation practice. She lifted it to her nose and inhaled the smell of religion, peace, antique honeysuckle, world travel, yoga, love, kindness, oneness. It smelled like…home. Not her home and not the house she grew up in. She couldn't identify it. But this scent, whatever it was, just smelled like home.

3

*"I asked God who I'm supposed to be
The stars smiled down on me
God answered in silent reverie
I said a prayer and fell asleep
I had a dream."
– Priscella Ahn*

Macy grew up in a busy bustling household. Her father was a mechanic and her mother was an art teacher. Carl was thick at 5'9" tall. He could easily palm a basketball. He was soft spoken, rarely angered, but when he spoke everyone listened. There was always music in their home. One never knew when a spontaneous dance party would break out. Carl often played The Eagles and danced behind Oona when she was busy at an easel. Their performance always ended with a dip. Macy loved their display of affection. Her brothers pretended to puke in their hands. *"Barf!"* They would hack dramatically.

Oona was a good singer. She hummed constantly while painting a canvas or refinishing furniture. She was modest about her voice except for singing with the church choir. No matter how much her brothers protested, they were all going to church on Sunday. It was non-negotiable for Carl. Macy didn't know why he was so insistent on this when she spied him napping during the sermon. His head would bob up and down as the preacher spoke. He just wanted the family to hear Oona sing. Sundays were the only time he didn't have grease on his hands.

Macy's Sunday School teacher had informed the class if they didn't witness to their friends, they would spend a fiery eternity in Hell with Satan. The teachings were fear-driven and required humiliation in the form of penance for being sinners. The actual church service moved in a similar direction.

Members of the congregation were urged at the end of each service to walk down the long aisle of the church toward the pulpit and stand to admit their sins. The sinners would hang their head in shame for a verse of "An Old Rugged Cross" as a reminder of what Jesus had to endure. The congregation would rush forward and place their hands on the sinner. Carl never budged from his seat and Oona never left her spot in the choir. Macy wondered why her parents didn't put their hands on the sinners. Probably because they didn't want to catch a case of the sins, she thought.

At six, Macy went to church for the last time. Her Sunday School teacher asked Macy to tell the class about her sins that week. Macy was pretty sure she shouldn't have kept the quarter she found on the ground just outside church that morning.

"What sins have you committed?" the teacher snapped.

Macy stood quietly in front of her peers. Her pale skin became blotchy as her nervousness grew.

"Do you think you're better than the rest of us? Well, you're a sinner. You need atonement from your evil acts. Tell the class your sins unless you want to go to Hell with snakes, spiders, rapists and murderers."

Macy shoved her hands in her sweater pocket and fingered the quarter. She felt everyone's eyes as she stood bowlegged, trembling in the corner. She needed to pee.

The teacher sputtered at Macy, approaching her, reciting verses over and over. "Romans 6:15: What then? Shall we sin because we are not under the law but under grace? By no means!" The teacher came inches from Macy's face. Macy could smell coffee on her breath.

Urine trickled down Macy's legs through her Harlequin pattern tights and onto her patent shoes. She pushed the teacher away and ran to the bathroom, flicking the quarter into the offering plate on the way.

Carl didn't say much on the way home. Macy was embarrassed. She saw her father yelling at the teacher above the bathroom stall. She wondered about the hypocrisy she saw each week. The words that came from the pulpit were vastly different than the behaviors she saw.

That afternoon Macy lay traumatized, gazing unfocused out her bedroom window. The wind blew a gust with just the right amount of force to move the old wind chimes that hung from their porch. Macy felt like she had seen this moment unfold before—as if it happened before. She pinched herself on the cheek. That too felt like it had happened previously. When Oona came into her room, the déjà vu had passed.

Oona sat on the edge of her bed. She tenderly twirled Macy's hair for several minutes before speaking. Her mother had a way of making the rest of the world disappear when she was around. Whoever Oona spent time with received her entire focus. It was a gift her mother gave freely and generously to anyone she encountered. "The copper in your hair reminds me of berries and wine," she said.

Macy thought about some kids in her Sunday School class, likening her to the devil because she was a redhead.

Her mother searched her face. "Mace?"

Macy looked up shyly at her mom. Oona gently cupped her chin and tilted her head so their eyes met.

"Mace. You just be you, okay?"

Macy's mother was the only one to shorten her name to Mace.

"Don't worry about your Sunday School teacher. We aren't going to church again."

Macy was relieved. "We're not? But what about—"

"You're a special girl, Macy Oona."

Macy started to cry. "What if I sin? When you and Daddy die, you'll go to Heaven and I'll go to H-E-L-L."

Oona laughed softly. "Oh, baby girl. Don't you worry your pretty little coppertone head."

Macy was confused. How could she not worry about God striking her with lightning and spending eternity with murderers?

Macy's mother came to her feet. "I'll tell you a secret." Oona leaned down like best friends exchanging a secret. "There is no H-E-L-L." She planted a kiss on Macy's nose, winked, and walked out of Macy's room.

Macy exhaled with great relief. She was so happy her mother told her the secret. That was the last time Macy ever pissed herself. The family never went to church again.

Oona and Carl were older when they gave birth to Macy. She was the youngest of her siblings. One day, Macy and Oona went out to lunch and the waitress commented, "How nice. Is your grandmother taking you out to lunch?" It was the first time Macy noticed Oona's age. Other moms didn't have gray hair.

Macy began creeping to the edge of her parents' bedroom door each night. The first time, she wasn't sure what she was listening for until she heard it. She was listening for signs of life. Breath. She wanted to know her parents had not died in their sleep. After she was satisfied they were alive, she crawled back in bed and slept.

Macy was plagued with dreams that left her baffled. She didn't always know how to interpret the vivid hints of past lives. She was never taught about reincarnation as a child. She would have been persecuted for that suggestion in her church. As an adult, Macy's dreams became more intense and made even less sense.

Macy dropped the lid of the trunk and released the tapestry from her nose with a long exhale. With a quick flip of the wrists, she spread the tapestry taut across the center of her bedroom and sat tall in the center of it. She was grounded…poised…honorable. She inhaled for several seconds and exhaled for even more. Constricting the back of her throat, she made a growling sound with each breath.

Since her mother told her the secret, Macy became determined not to use the church's teachings as her compass. Every Sunday after they quit the church, Macy and Oona would sit on the floor stretching, chatting, and doing yoga together.

"Mace, all you have to do is pay attention to how you feel in your solar plexus to make the best decisions for yourself." Oona placed her hand on Macy's stomach. "It's what we call instincts. Your gut will tell you whatever you need to know if you learn to listen. It's okay to feel first and then make decisions in life. Ignoring your instincts will cause a tightening pain in here." Oona moved her hand above Macy's belly button. Macy knew her mother was wise. She could feel it.

When Macy's family surrounded the dinner table, Macy would take the time to memorize each face. She was filled with love for all of them. Macy's brothers would kick each other under the table. Inevitably someone would spit green beans into the bottom of their milk and hope to remain anonymous. She had a quiet understanding that the only thing certain about life was its impermanence. She embraced the chaos and disorganization. Carl always helped in the kitchen. He loved to crack eggs and make sounds of vomiting as he poured out the yoke. It was a joke that never got old. From a young age, Macy knew life was an ephemeral pleasure.

Macy went through a vinyasa flow to warm her body. Teaching gymnastics to elementary school kids three days a week kept her strong and limber. Although she wouldn't admit it to Daniel, she was glad he was so straight-laced. Since she had stopped smoking pot, she had more endurance than ever before. She ran an eight-minute mile. She had never considered herself to be an athlete. Athletes were people who were born and bred to compete. Macy was missing that gene. She never cared about winning, but she was healthy.

4

"You look so wonderful in your dress
I love your hair like that
The way it falls on the side of your neck
Down your shoulders and back."
– Ed Sheeran

At 6'6", Daniel was muscular enough not to be lanky. His hair was yellow blond, short, parted perfectly sweeping to the right. His eyes were electric blue. People joked that he was the athletic version of the Ken doll. His passion for good health was a huge contrast to Macy's stoner habits—he never took a day off from running, biking, or swimming. He received a full scholarship to NC State for his talent, but during his first year, he tore his ACL at practice and required surgery. His injury helped him re-evaluate the pressures and demands of playing college ball. He relented his scholarship soon after and focused on his studies. His roommates moved to California on a whim right after college. Daniel moved back in with his parents but it became difficult for him to stay there. He moved to California with his buddy, Pat, and got a good job developing software for cell phones. He enjoyed the single life until he met Macy at a bar one night.

Both of Daniel's sisters graduated from NC State as well. They knew what degree they were seeking as early as their freshman year. Daniel's younger sister was a nurse and the older was an accountant, like their father. Daniel's father was disappointed that Daniel couldn't finish college as a member of the basketball team. He rarely missed an opportunity to remind Daniel about blowing his scholarship.

A former football player, Mr. Westcott sustained an injury that led to his constant furrowed brow. At 6'6", his stomach protruded over his belt. During the Christmas break immediately following Daniel's injury, he condescendingly berated him in front of his oldest sister's boyfriend. "I just got slapped with three years of tuition thanks to gimpy over here. Have you even picked a major yet? Sheesh, there's one rotten egg in every bunch. Two out of three, I guess." He elbowed Daniel as if this was their inside joke. Daniel stayed in his room the rest of the break playing video games.

Mr. Westcott required a plethora of prescription medication for allergies and other disorders. He wore the hypersensitivities like medals. He dramatically suffered when anyone wore perfume or used strong soap, hair spray, or even scented deodorant. He was the proud owner of every inhaler, breathing treatment, nebulizer, and bronchodilator on the market. He waved his hand over them like showing merchandise on *The Price is Right*.

Daniel warned Macy before bringing her home. He encouraged her not to shake his father's hand and to be as scent-free as possible. When Macy shook his hand for the first time, Mr. Westcott went to the kitchen sink and scrubbed furiously up to his elbows with a scouring pad as if disinfecting for surgery. While he patted dry with gauze pads, he oriented Macy on how he could get hives just from smelling her. He educated her on mood disorders, eating disorders, OCD, PTSD, ADHD. The only disorder Macy detected was BS.

Mrs. Westcott was a tall, frail woman. She would take one bite of her dinner and complain she was distended. She wore turtlenecks that exposed her vertebrae but never wore the same outfit twice.

The Westcotts employed a nurse to help with the chores of caring for Mr. Westcott. Her tasks included refilling sanitizer gel in all of Mr. Westcott's sanitizing stations and keeping fresh socks on all of the door handles in the house, as Mr. Westcott did not like to touch doorknobs.

Mrs. Westcott wore designer suits to their country club where she could be found playing bridge every afternoon with other socialites. When her children were young, they were always dressed in high-end clothes. Daniel winced when he recalled playing basketball in a stiffly starched shirt after school. Mrs. Westcott rarely attempted physical contact with her kids. Even in their family portrait she stood like a statue, hands by her side. When Daniel tried to engage in a conversation with her about a movie he had seen called *Back to the Future*, Mrs. Westcott's gaze moved away from him. When he finished his question, she was silent. "Were you done with your story?" she asked. Daniel noted that she often had a far-away look in her eyes as if her mind was somewhere else. Eventually he stopped talking to her.

Mrs. Westcott had a ritual before bed. She would curl her hair, spray it, and cover it with a plastic cap. The family rarely ate dinner together. Mrs. Westcott cooked for Mr. Westcott, but the children's activities kept her from cooking for them. The two dined in the formal dining room. The oldest daughter would often make scrambled eggs and toss her leftovers onto a plate for Daniel. Mrs. Westcott perpetuated her husband's neurosis by telling everyone within earshot about the latest development on the horizon. When Mr. Westcott spoke of his disorders, she always stopped what she was doing. "Tsk, tsk, tsk." She would offer a moment of silence before moving on.

Even among themselves, Daniel's sisters didn't smile, joke, or even fight often. One occasion he overheard his sisters refer to their father as the life plunger who sucked the life out of a room and that he was the fattest anorexic on record. Daniel covered his mouth to laugh, but their tone was somber.

Each morning when Mr. Westcott woke up, he rang a bell for Mrs. Westcott to come assist him. She'd turn his TV on to his favorite financial channel. He lay in his bed, arms stretched out. Mrs. Westcott would then remove the previous day's prescription body lotion with a device that resembled a cheese knife as he watched for the latest news on the NASDAQ. At 5:00 each night, the nurse was dismissed and Mrs. Westcott took over the duties for her husband. Mrs. Westcott would serve him two glasses of single barrel scotch whisky, several shot glasses with pills in the bottom, and anesthetic wet wipes.

Mr. Westcott would knock the shot glass on the metal kitchen table three times and chug his pills.

Their home was ornately decorated and they used fine china for every meal. Each night after the two ate dinner, Mr. Westcott exited the dining room by flipping the light switch off and on three times and immediately smothering his hands in clear sanitizing gel appropriately situated next to the light switch. At bedtime, with her shower cap over her neatly pressed hair, Mrs. Westcott reapplied the lotion for him. She covered his large belly, tucked the sheets under his back, and fit his nasal cannula in his nostrils so he could breathe pure oxygen while he slept.

5

"There she stood in the doorway
I heard the mission bell
Then I was thinking to myself
this could be Heaven
or this could be Hell."
– The Eagles

Daniel and his roommates settled into Poway, California. They could get to San Diego within thirty minutes. They partied every weekend. One of their favorite stops was Marlene Renée's Bar, open 10:00 PM to 6:00 AM. Like a skate rink, it had a wood dance floor in the middle of the room. It was perfect for checking out the girls from the perimeter. It frequently hosted bachelorette and divorce parties.

Macy's band finished their last set and the DJ was taking over. He started by playing Salt and Pepa's "Push It." Daniel's roommate, Pat, approached Macy first.

"Hey, I saw you playing guitar. You're pretty good," he slurred.

"Thanks," Macy said quietly.

The guys in her band gave her a hard time for going home right after their gigs. She usually packed her Fender immediately after the last song. This is why—drunk annoying men.

"I promised to hang out with the guys after the gig for a bit. I'd better go catch up with them. Nice chatting," she said, easing away.

Daniel watched the exchange and he liked her immediately. She stuck out. Most girls here traveled in leather-clad packs. Macy had bracelets up to her elbows, a long loose skirt, and russet dreadlocks down to her butt. Everything about her seemed to flow loosely. At 5'5" she was radiant, confident, and reeked of pot.

Macy's skin was a milky contrast to her ruby hair and emerald eyes. The tattoos on her upper shoulder were visible, as was her nose ring, catching the light. Her untamed copper dreadlocks lifted off her scalp like Medusa. She was everything Daniel wasn't. He couldn't take his eyes off her. He watched her across the room, careful not to get caught. He was positioned perfectly so she couldn't see him staring. There was a quiet assurance about the way she moved her hips. When she laughed she tilted her head back and clutched her stomach. She pulled a joint from her bra and took three hits off it—boom, boom, boom—one right after the other. She held the marijuana in her lungs as she motioned to pass it as if offering a stick of gum. Daniel laughed out loud at her audacity. Everything about her felt boldly cool. He was captivated.

Pat stumbled up to Daniel, sloshing his beer. "Hey buddy!" He slapped Daniel's back and looked up slightly at him. "Whatcha doin' over here? Come join the party." He dragged Daniel over toward her. A few feet away from her now, Daniel could see her piercing green eyes even better.

Daniel rarely did anything illegal. The few times he had smoked pot, he crashed on the couch after eating a bag of Cheetos. Macy seemed fueled by it. She prided herself on how many different ways she could smoke pot. She once used a green pepper as a bong and a Pepsi can as a bowl. Sometimes she cut the bottom off a gallon of milk and filled her kitchen sink with water. Replacing the lid with tin foil, she placed weed in the makeshift metal bowl and lit it. She slowly lifted the gallon as she lit, causing the smoke to be suctioned into the container. Once full and almost lifted to the surface, she removed the top, put her mouth around the opening, and quickly pressed the gallon down to the bottom while inhaling.

Daniel and Pat moved in closer to Macy. The smell of weed permeated the air. Pat, who was barely standing upright, told Daniel about Macy's gig. "Dude, before you got here, she sang a version of 'Hotel California' that was dope."

Daniel was annoyed at his roommate for getting so hammered. Pat was supposed to drive everyone back to Poway but Daniel wasn't going to let him. Just as he was going to suggest they leave, Pat tipped over the rail and tugged on Macy's shirt.

"Daniel, this is my good friend. We go *waaay* back. Wassyur name again?"

Macy looked slightly annoyed at Pat but Daniel took the opportunity and ran with it. "Hi, I'm Daniel. You'll have to excuse my friend." He waved Pat off to the side. Daniel's tall frame towered over Macy.

"So, you two go so far back he doesn't know your name?" Daniel asked, attempting to play along. She smiled effortlessly at his attempt.

The two laughed and the conversation flowed. Soon her band members started leaving. Tommy, the drummer, came over to her.

"Hey, you good or you want me to hang around?"

"I'm good. I'm gonna catch a cab in a few minutes."

"Right on. Glad you finally stayed out with us. See, we're not that bad!"

They hugged and he shook Daniel's hand.

"Night, man. Make sure she gets out okay." Tommy held Daniel's gaze a second longer in reinforcement. "Really man, make sure she gets a cab safely."

"Will do." Daniel tipped his head at Tommy as if he understood. Macy was different.

Daniel and Macy bellied up to the bar and talked until 3:00 AM. He was from a small town in North Carolina. He had two sisters, graduated from NC State, and moved to California for a job developing software applications. Daisy Duke was his celebrity crush and he had taken the Lake George polar plunge. Macy laughed easily at his jokes while he maintained her interest for hours. He was not her typical suitor. He was clean-cut, preppy, handsome, sensible, smart…. Macy's intellectual achievement was knowing a hundred ways to refer to marijuana: spliff, joint, cannabis, weed, doobie, bud, joint, reefer, roach, hemp, hashish, dope, herb, ganja, hash, Maryjane, grass, bhang, cheeba, kush, shwag, wacky tabaky, left-handed cigarettes, skunk, devil's lettuce, hippie cabbage, dirty parsley, diggity dank.

As soon as another slow song played, Daniel asked Macy to dance.

"I don't dance much," Macy answered, embarrassed.

"I'll lead," Daniel offered with his hand. He led Macy to the dance floor, picked her up, and set her feet right on top of his. She laughed as he counted the steps. "One two three, one two three."

Macy couldn't remember the last time she had been out this late. She suddenly became restless thinking about her dog back home. The pooch had not been let out in hours. She quickly grabbed her bag.

"But wait, I did all the talking. Tell me about you," he said with a plea.

She spotted a bar napkin from the dispenser and jotted her information: *Macy 444-813-0926.*

"That's it? I get your number? Can I take you home? I won't try anything, promise. Wait, I promised your friend I'd walk you to a cab." He trailed behind her.

Outside, she whistled loudly with her fingers. As if waiting in the alley all night just for Macy, a cab pulled up immediately. She threw the door open but stopped short. Turning back, she gave him a feather light kiss on the cheek and jumped into the cab.

"Nice to meetcha," she said out the taxi window. He stood holding the limp napkin in hand and hoped it was her real number.

Guy code states you should wait one day before calling the girl you are interested in. So, Daniel did the right thing. It was her real number. Their courtship lasted exactly one year from the day they met. They have that napkin framed in a box somewhere in their new garage.

The first time Daniel went to Macy's apartment, she opened the door and exhaled, "Whew, I knew I liked your energy, but your face is…well, actually cuter than I remembered."

Daniel smiled in relief.

The ugliest dog Daniel had ever seen in his life padded up.

"Meet Mukha." Macy gestured at the yippee dog scratching at Daniel's leg. He leaned down pretending to be enamored by the dog.

Her 400-square foot studio was in an old warehouse in La Jolla. The apartment was open and stretched concrete from front to back. It smelled like a marijuana greenhouse. Through the open bathroom door, Daniel could see a glob of toothpaste on the mirror and dirty clothes on the floor. Macy had tchotchkes, knick-knacks, and trinkets everywhere. Incense rose from a stick in the corner. Madeleine Peyroux's jazzy voice came from the stereo. Macy hummed along as she poured them each a glass of wine and packed a bowl. Daniel was impressed with her humming. She sounded just like the recording.

"Wanna get high?" she asked him within seconds of his arrival.

"Ummm…okay," he said. He didn't inhale.

6

*"I will become yours and
You will become mine.
I choose you."*
— Sara Barielles

Daniel and Macy dated for three months before they slept together. It was a Friday night and Daniel's office was having an app software release party. She wore a crushed burgundy velvet jacket with bell sleeves. She pulled her dreadlocks into a loose ponytail. Macy was nervous to meet his co-workers. She appreciated that he had a career.

Daniel enjoyed having her on his arm that night. To his surprise, nobody commented on her dreadlocks or the fact that they were so obviously opposite. In fact, one of his co-workers took him aside to say how the two balanced each other.

"I am happier than I've ever been. She's definitely the one," Daniel told his colleague.

That night, Macy and Daniel made love for the first time. Their relationship had moved to the next level.

Macy and Daniel's lives began to merge. Daniel was a constant presence at her gigs. Eventually people knew him as well as her. He liked being known as Macy's boyfriend. The free drinks weren't bad either. Their friends met and became friends—even Pat.

"It sucks that my only single friend is taken now, but at least I'm the wise one who introduced them," Pat used to joke. Daniel spent more time at her place in La Jolla and less with the boys in Poway. "Dude, you're taking her dog to work with you? You are seriously pussy whipped!" Pat teased.

Macy adopted her dog, Mukha, just before she dropped out of college and enrolled in yoga school. One day after she finished a yoga class at the spiritual center, she saw a flyer that

read, "Rescue dogs. Otherwise they are headed to the SPCA."
At the time she lived in a tiny apartment with girlfriends. She
played guitar at a coffee shop around the corner, waited tables
at night, and earned her yoga certification on the weekends.
Everything was in walking distance to her apartment, so she
didn't own a car. She had to make enough money to pay rent
and a third of the utilities each month. She calculated her
expenses. Once she started teaching yoga she would have
enough money to get her own place and a dog.

She pulled one of the tags off the bottom of the flyer.
With her roommate's blessings, she caught a ride up to the dog
farm a week later.

The address was close to Torrey Pines. Macy was
expecting a more established-looking building but they drove
to a dilapidated trailer in the middle of nowhere. A lady
resembling Tammy Faye Baker emerged from the rickety trailer
door with a cigarette hanging out of her mouth. She had large
sprayed hair, tight leather pants that tapered all the way to her
ankles, and red high heels.

"Hey y'all." She spoke with the cigarette still attached to
her lips. The voice that came out of the woman was Southern.
"We've got lots of puppies ready to go!" she said, surveying the
crowd of animals that assembled at her feet. One hand was on
her hip, the other motioned toward them as if she was
modeling the inventory. "Wanda down the street, she don't
keep her dawg on no leash. He humps anything that walks, so
poor Annabelle got knocked up again. So, we're practically
giving them away for $50. I've already given each of them a
flea bath treatment—that's on the house. Which one do you
want?" Tammy Faye was ready to close the sale.

Macy looked down at the puppies. They were adorable.
Macy bent down and stroked one. They jumped, climbed, and
nipped excitedly. Just then, Macy could see inside Tammy
Faye's trailer. Up on the kitchen table strapped to a harness
stood an emaciated dog with a shame collar around his neck.

Mugs had an underbite that snagged his upper lip, leaving the bottom tooth exposed. The collar was huge on his little face. His ribs were exposed when he inhaled and his legs were shaking to hold his body up. Pus oozed from a wound under his eye.

"What happened to"—Macy looked down to identify his sex organs—"him?" She motioned inside the trailer.

Tammy Faye glanced over her shoulder. "Tha-a-at?" she said with extra syllables while pointing her long red acrylic nail at the dog. "That's Mugs. Jimmy calls him that because he's so ugly. Ha! Ain't he ugly? Don't he got an ugly mug?"

Tammy Faye used her hip to open the door wider as she flicked her cigarette onto the dirt. The cigarette grazed one of the puppies. Immediately, she took another cigarette out of her bra and lit it, taking a long drag. "Jimmy's got a temper. Jimmy lives down yonder…works all day, comes home and expects ol' Mugs here to keep his bladder. When he don't, Jimmy gets mad as a hornet. The old dawg turns up here. I told Jimmy I'd come let Mugs out to pee but he don't want me snooping in his house. Burns my biscuit! Probably afraid I'd take a nip of his gin. Ha!" Her laugh tore through the air, making Macy jump.

Macy's face felt sunburned and prickly as Tammy Faye yammered on about Mugs being chained in the rain.

"I'll take him," Macy blurted out with more emotion than she intended.

Tammy Faye eyeballed her as if she had lost her mind. Her painted eyebrows were in higher arches now. "See that infection? He's in bad shape. Plus, he's Jimmy's dawg. I can't just give away Jimmy's dawg."

Macy felt a protectiveness spew from her insides. "Well, you can't give him back to that asshole just to do it again. You're enabling the cycle to continue." Macy was pissed. "I know you're trying to help him, but you can't give him back to that man." The words flew out of her mouth.

Tammy Faye looked like she'd been slapped in the face. "I'm the reason this dog is even alive, Missy." Tammy stood. Her lip curled under. Macy's ride excused herself and waited in the car.

Tammy Faye took a long tug off her cigarette that was almost all ash now. She walked over toward Mugs and exhaled near his face. Macy winced. "Look, I have some tips in my pocket." Macy pulled out a wad of ones and fives.

After a long pause, Tammy Faye spoke again. "Well, I reckon we can work something out. You know—for Mug's sake." Tammy Faye unlatched the dog's noose and he fell to the table, where Macy's reflex was to catch him. The two stood facing each other. Tammy Faye swiped the cash and reached for a fresh cigarette. "Bless your heart," she said and closed the door.

Back at her apartment that night, Macy and her girlfriends gathered around the pooch. Having used what was supposed to be her rent money to buy him, Macy used her credit card and called a vet who made emergency house calls. The vet gave Macy needles and syringes to medicate Mugs with antibiotics. She was shocked to learn he was only around three years old. He was infested with fleas and had tapeworms. The vet showed Macy how to pull his skin up around his neck and administer the medication.

The first time she gave him a shot, he snapped at her. It was the one and only time he didn't trust her.

"You can trust me, buddy. You know what, Mugs? You're going to have a new life. I know you've been through a lot. How about a new name to honor your past, but something for your future too? Let's see.... How about Scrappy?"

The dog sat looking at her.

"Nah, how about Rocky because you're a fighter and a champ?"

Again, no reaction from the dog.

She sat back and looked at his face. His lip caught onto his lower tooth. Macy thought he had the cutest face she'd ever seen. "How about Mukha! It means *face* in Sanskrit!"

Mugs stood up, scratched her hand, and wagged his tail.

"Mukha it is!"

As she slowly earned his trust, she gained a companion who would never leave her side.

Daniel knew how much Mukha meant to Macy, so when he proposed, he wrapped a ribbon around the dog's collar and threaded an engagement ring through it. When Macy leaned over to attach a leash for Mukha's afternoon walk, she was shocked to see the sparkling diamond attached. She turned around to find Daniel on one knee.

7

"She's gettin' you right
Knows what you like
And pours it on like gasoline."
– David Nail

Although Daniel and his roommates shared a house, it was more organized than Macy's. Every item had its place. Daniel's CDs were in alphabetical order. His closet looked like a color-coordinated rainbow. He offered to help her give order to her home, as organizational skills were not her strongest. A few months before the wedding, Macy had yet to buy a gown.

Daniel and Macy flew to North Carolina to meet the preacher who would ordain their wedding. Mrs. Westcott was horrified to find out Macy had not yet purchased a dress. Mrs. Westcott encouraged her future daughter-in-law to reconsider her look for the wedding day.

"You want to look proper on your wedding day. Maybe something with sleeves. You will regret having your tattoos exposed in your wedding picture later when you've finally matured. You'll need a classic veil. My hairdresser will help you with your twisty things. And for Pete's sake, take that hoop out of your nose that day. Our entire rolodex of friends will be at the wedding," she said, her voice thick with her Southern drawl.

Mrs. Westcott was firm that each of Macy's bridesmaids should be dressed identically. She encouraged Macy to have her friends buy their dresses from a wedding shop in Wilmington for the price of $450. Macy knew her bridesmaids were on a budget. She also knew they all had different figures and personalities. She couldn't pick one dress for all of them. Macy decided not to have bridesmaids at all. Instead, she asked Oona to stand with her as her matron of honor.

In an effort to keep the peace, Macy was passive and agreed on a traditional veil but she didn't buy a dress that week. The next week Macy and Daniel were back in San Diego walking through the farmer's market as usual. They were sampling chips and salsas when Macy looked down the street and saw a silk ivory dress hanging from a vendor's tent. The tag blew in the wind. As they approached, Macy was thrilled to read in red marker *$79*. It was floor length with just a few pearl embellishments.

"You'll make it look like a million bucks. Just don't tell my mom how cheap it was." They laughed and Macy bought the dress.

8

"You say I'm crazy
cause you don't think I know what you've done
but when you call me baby
I know I'm not the only one."
— Sam Smith

When Macy and Daniel were ready to start a family, they decided to move to North Carolina.

"I can't believe you're actually moving back," Pat said to Daniel.

"It's a purely financial decision," Daniel assured.

East Coast living expenses and both sets of parents available to babysit made the decision easier. Daniel planned it out financially. It worked on paper as long as Macy continued to work through her pregnancy. Daniel's father had carefully forecasted the birth of his kids similarly in a spreadsheet. Daniel remembered his father documenting every penny spent. Macy was used to living paycheck to paycheck. Her parents made a modest income but she never felt deprived. Because she sang at the bars at night and taught yoga during the day, Macy was relaxed about the ebb and flow of money. She gave generous gifts to friends and tipped well when she dined out. Macy respected his sensibility, but teased Daniel about having the baby's college tuition saved before they even conceived.

Macy got pregnant on their first try. Daniel gave out cigars to his friends. "My boys can swim!" he gloated.

Macy loved being pregnant. The first time she felt the faint flutter of the baby move, she was singing at a gig. When she realized what it was, it came out of her mouth and into the microphone. "I just felt the baby move!" she shouted to strangers in a bar. At seventeen weeks, they found out the baby was a boy.

Macy continued to teach yoga and work at the gymnasium but she stopped singing at gigs when her belly began to show. At twenty-three weeks pregnant, fatigue was setting in. She usually went to bed by 9:00 PM.

She woke close to midnight one night and Daniel was not in bed. She peered out of the bedroom looking for him. She was surprised when she found him in his office.

"Hey babe," she murmured.

He jumped and quickly turned off the computer monitor before she could see what he was browsing. "Hi sweetheart. I was just coming to bed."

Macy's instincts buzzed.

The next day Macy searched the computer's history and discovered an email from Pat to Daniel.

Check out this one...Vicky Vegas.

Macy clicked on the attachment and discovered a porn website. She didn't know why it bothered her so much. A lot of men looked at porn, she knew. She certainly wasn't surprised at Pat, but it bothered her that Daniel was looking. He had never expressed an interest in it before.

She looked down at her swelling body. Her fingers looked like sausages. She felt more unattractive than ever. She no longer fit into any of her regular clothes but maternity clothes looked too big. She felt fat.

Macy explored more of the computer's history and found that Daniel had visited several porn sites. Macy clicked on each link. The women were thin, tall, and olive complexioned—everything Macy wasn't. It caused a pit of anger in her pelvic floor. She could not shake the fact that he was looking at other women while she was carrying his baby.

There were chat room links, photos, even a poorly produced video. Macy tortured herself by watching the video four times. The scene was of a man on a business trip walking into his hotel room to stumble on a hooker who accidently checked into the man's room. She didn't understand how anyone could be aroused at the skit. It was amateur at best.

Hot anger flared up inside Macy. She thought about replying to Pat, *"Don't send Daniel any more of your garbage entertainment."* But she clicked out instead. She was exhausted.

Daniel had to work late. Macy stewed all day. She watched the video again. She investigated more women like Vicky Vegas. Nina New York, Minnesota Mina—their names were as creative as their homemade video clips. She felt an odd sense of sympathy for the women on the websites. What would they do when the porn industry rejected them for their overfilled implants because they were old?

Macy couldn't help but to think about her Grammy. She was an endowed woman whose breasts hung heavy and low to her waist. She was constantly hunched over from their weight. Her last few years were spent in a wheelchair, where Macy sensed Grammy was relieved to no longer have to lug the weight of her breasts around. Hugs were awkward, getting past one huge lump of saggy boob. Maybe there was a niche market for men who sought women with huge boobs hanging down to their navels. Macy wondered if her husband was one of those men.

Macy tried to soothe herself with a warm bath. She pampered herself by painting her nails and listening to guided meditations. She dressed for bed in her favorite nightgown.

She was still awake when Daniel finally arrived home. Her imagination was working overtime. When Daniel tiptoed into their room, he had no idea Macy was awake lying in the dark stewing. She sat up, turned on her lamp, and confronted Daniel about the porn she found on his computer.

Daniel stumbled with his excuses. He was drunk, Macy realized. His face flushed red.

"Macy, I know you're upset, but I don't know a man who doesn't look at porn at some point in his life. You're overreacting because you're hormonal."

Macy's milky complexion was red and blotchy as she held back tears. The more he defended himself, the angrier she got.

"So it's my fault that I'm overreacting at you looking at a porn site when I'm pregnant with your baby? Am I overreacting about you coming in stumbling drunk while you were, quote, 'working late'?"

She jumped out of bed, slapped her bare feet down the stairs, and grabbed her keys. Before Daniel could stop her, she was outside in her nightgown getting into the car. She tore out of the driveway.

Macy didn't know where she was going, but her blood was boiling, and that's all that seemed to matter. She headed in the direction of Oona and Carl's home forty-five minutes away. She didn't think she would tell them what happened, she just wanted to be with people who loved her unconditionally.

As she drove, she replayed Daniel's words over in her head. She hated that he called her hormonal. She thought she would become calmer as she drove, but she was halfway to her parents' house and she still wanted to scream. Her hands clenched the steering wheel.

She passed an old Southern bed and breakfast with huge magnolia trees outside. The inn caught her eye. She turned her head to look closer as she contemplated getting a room there for the night.

When she looked back to the street, she saw a woman in the middle of the road. The woman looked like she could have been Macy's twin. Macy intended to slam on the brakes but instead, she hit the gas.

She felt the car smack an object.

Everything went black.

Macy woke up to the feeling of fluid gushing from between her legs. She opened her eyes and there was a mask over her face and ambulance lights flickered over her head.

9

"Settle down, it'll all be clear
Don't pay no mind to the demons
They fill you with fear."
– Phillip Phillips

As Macy came to consciousness, she realized she was strapped to a gurney. She was being placed in the back of the ambulance. Daniel was there, rattling off information about Macy's pregnancy. Macy's amniotic sac had been ruptured in the impact.

Macy rehashed the events of the night. Her fight with Daniel over the porn seemed so insignificant now. Their baby's life was in flux. She was being taken to a hospital where there was a neonatal intensive care unit. If there was a heartbeat, the baby would be too young to survive outside of the womb. Why had she been so hasty with her unborn child inside her?

The voices of the paramedics around her quickly developed a plan to give Macy a shot of surfactant steroids to jumpstart the baby's lung development. One of the EMS workers quickly cleaned the gash over Macy's eye and put a butterfly bandage over it but blood continued to ooze. An IV was inserted and she was taken to UNC Children's Hospital.

A team of doctors met her as they arrived. One of the doctors softly warned her, "The impact caused your sac to rupture. Most women with a broken bag of waters go into labor within twenty-four hours or get an infection that requires immediate delivery. Your baby still has a heartbeat, so you'll stay at UNC until you deliver. It's my duty to warn you that if your baby comes now, it has less than a twenty-five percent chance of surviving." The doctor patted Macy's arm and turned to the nurses with a grim look.

Macy began to shake in shock. Daniel was bewildered.

One of the nurses held a long needle just out of Macy's vision. Daniel's eyes widened at the length of the needle.

"Roll to your side, honey," the nurse said. "It's going to burn and shoot heat down your leg, but just when you think you can't take anymore, it will be over."

The nurse stabbed Macy with the syringe before she could comprehend anything. The nurse's description was accurate. Macy panted; the mixture of fear and pain was overwhelming. Another attendant slathered jelly on her stomach and strapped monitors across her midsection. Macy received a crash course on premature birth survival rates—the statistics were grim. The handicaps of those who did survive were staggering.

Macy was taken to the operating room where she was greeted by a medical team ready to perform an emergency cesarean section. They explained that once the bag of waters ruptures, delivery is usually imminent. The lack of amniotic fluid puts the baby under stress, forcing labor, usually via cesarean.

One of the nurses, Jerry, measured Macy's vitals. "The baby doesn't appear to be in distress from the impact or from the patient losing consciousness. FHR steady at 157." Jerry turned to Macy and explained the baby's heart rate was at the higher range of normal but strong.

Daniel busied himself by calling Oona and Carl.

Jerry gave the same report thirty minutes later. Another half hour passed and the baby's vital signs were still stable.

Jerry comforted Macy. "This is positive news. Every hour gained could change the outcome of things for your baby. The longer you can stay pregnant, the better. I read your chart; you've already received a shot of surfactant. In twenty-four hours, we can give you another one. That will be helpful in the baby's lung development. We just need you to stay pregnant that long, okay sweetie?"

Macy felt like everything was buzzing around her. She appreciated Jerry for simplifying the information for her. Jerry touched her hand with compassion and turned to talk with the doctor.

A decision was made to put Macy in a regular hospital room until the baby's vital signs changed. Jerry and the team of nurses wheeled Macy to a private room. Every time Macy moved even slightly, a stream of fluid trickled out between her legs. A whiteboard attached to the back of the bathroom door in Macy's new room had the words *To do list: Don't move. Stay pregnant.* Jerry smiled at Macy as he wrote it. "Now, these are nurse's orders. We're going to keep you attached to the monitors. As soon as anything changes, we'll get the baby out. I hope that doesn't happen for a long time. I'll be back to stitch up that nice gash over your eye…unless you'd prefer to wait for a plastic surgeon."

"You can stitch it," Macy said with a weak grin. It was the first time she had really spoken.

Jerry smiled. "Well, good then, I'm practically a plastic surgeon. Okay, not really. I barely graduated nursing school, but I'm gay, so I'm practically an artist. Okay, not really." He laughed at his own joke. "Do *not* get up from the bed." He winked at Macy and handed her a bedpan and left the room.

Macy and Daniel were left to digest their reality. Macy couldn't believe she had just been in a car accident and caused this to happen to her baby. Everything was so normal yesterday. She wanted to rewind time. Daniel held Macy while she cried.

"I'm sorry I did this to our baby. I can't believe I let my emotions take control."

Daniel consoled Macy. "If I hadn't been such a jerk, you wouldn't have left."

They were both contrite.

"Daniel, what happened to the lady in the street? She looked just like me. Oh God, did I hit her?" Macy's heart started to race. She pushed herself up from the bed. A monitor sounded.

Daniel consoled Macy. "Settle down. Be still. No one said anything about a woman. You have a concussion, just take it easy."

Macy dozed in and out of consciousness. Jerry came in at the end of his shift and explained that she was doing great. The team decided to downgrade their monitoring. "You're officially on bed rest," Jerry informed. "You can get up to use the restroom but that's it. Instead of keeping the fetal heart rate monitor around your tummy, someone will come in every two hours to measure the baby's heartbeat. I'll be back tomorrow and I hope you're still pregnant."

The next day consisted of sonograms, blood draws, pelvic exams, intercom announcements, beeps, bells, and alarms. One day became one week and one week became three. Macy developed bedsores from staying in bed all day and night. She was uncomfortable but maintained her resolve to do all she could to help her baby survive.

Daniel stayed in the hospital with Macy most nights. After about a week, it was becoming apparent that the baby wasn't going to come immediately. Jerry reminded her to relax and enjoy her time being pregnant since no one knew how long that would last.

Daniel's office was forty-five minutes away. After the first week in the hospital, Macy insisted Daniel go back to work. Finances were tight, so he agreed.

Macy felt like everyone was staring at her waiting for the baby to suddenly come. Oona came to the hospital every day and sat with her. The two women played board games, told stories of the past, laughed, cried, meditated, and prayed. Macy thought a lot about what it meant to be a mother. Here she was, in her late twenties, and her mother was still taking care of her. They were visited by a rabbi, a priest, and other clergymen. They had interesting discussions about religion. They made beaded bracelets with inspirational words on them for the night staff. She sketched drawings and wrote poetry and songs every day.

During the second week at UNC, Macy's father, Carl, surprised her by bringing her guitar. It was technically not allowed in the hospital because it wasn't sterile. But Jerry helped them bend the rules. She and Carl used to sing hymns together from the crazy church. That was all she remembered singing with him. Those were the first things she strummed on her guitar: "Amazing Grace," "What a Friend We Have in Jesus," "How Great Thou Art." Carl had a strong tenor voice but he could also bellow rich bass notes too.

Macy looked at her sweet father sitting on the side of her hospital bed. Now his brown hair was almost completely silver, but he still had smooth light skin like Macy. His eyes were a piercing green just like hers. The duo grew a crowd of nurses outside her hospital room to listen.

Four weeks after her water broke, the staff was buzzing about Macy maintaining her pregnancy. Jerry even came by on his day off. During their hours together, Macy had confided that she loved North Carolina barbecue. So, Jerry brought his partner, Steve, to meet Macy. He introduced her as the woman who was going to set a world record. "Girlfriend, we were placing bets on you. The longest anyone has stayed pregnant in this situation was seven days. No one thought you'd last this long. I lost $20 on the eighth day." Jerry winked. His presence put Macy at ease. She laughed easily around him and his partner as they ate the barbeque and hush puppies.

Jerry casually asked if she had considered taking photos of the baby when he was born. Macy had not thought of the implications. She didn't even have many photos of her pregnant belly. Because her sac was ruptured, her stomach had deflated some now. It was only at her last appointment that she found out she was having a boy. She thought she would have more time for things like photos. They didn't even have a crib yet. She thought they would have several months to prepare for their son's arrival, but nothing was going as planned.

Macy's strong reaction to Jerry's question surprised her. She decided she would take pictures of the baby. Whether the baby survived or died, nothing would change the fact that from the moment she gave birth, she would be a mother.

Daniel stayed at the hospital on the weekends. Jerry brought him a cot with blankets and pillows. Macy had not been left alone in four weeks. The intercom in her room constantly buzzed with voices, the door rarely stayed closed for longer than ten minutes. Macy relished the few moments she was alone to appeal to her guardian angels and spirit guides. Pleading on behalf of her unborn child, she would chant in meditation. Guilt enveloped her like a thick cloud. She asked for forgiveness from her unborn son. She wondered every day about the woman in the street. No one had any explanation for that. She hated herself for getting in the car and driving when she was so upset. She asked for the divine feminine Mother Mary to heal her body so that her baby would live.

It was September and Macy had been on bed rest for more than a month at UNC. Summer was transitioning to fall. It was eighty-eight degrees the night she was admitted to the hospital but it was a crisp fifty-nine degrees on this particular day. Daniel was out for his run and Macy was trying to nap but she was nauseated and horribly uncomfortable. The nausea became cramps. It finally dawned on her. *Oh my God, I'm having contractions.* She waited until Daniel returned to tell the doctors. As soon as he walked into her hospital room, she hit the emergency call button.

A team of medical professionals filed into Macy's room like an infantry. This was the moment everyone had been expecting for several weeks. Now that it was finally here, everyone except Macy and Daniel knew what to do. Daniel got on the phone to call Oona and Carl when the doctor on call arrived. The physician, Dr. Rhen, had been there for a couple of Saturdays so Macy recognized her face. Dr. Rhen had a team of residents with her. With a room full of people, the doctor examined Macy's condition. She peeked over Macy's knees and flicked her rubber glove around her wrist, making a snapping noise.

"Mrs. Westcott"—(every time Macy heard someone refer to her like that she still looked for Daniel's mom)—"your baby is ready to come. The head is starting to crown. We don't want him to experience distress. We're going to get you to the operating room right now for an emergency cesarean." She motioned to the student residents holding clipboards. They feverishly scribbled notes. Everyone burst into motion.

Daniel had just hung up the phone and asked the doctor, "Wait, what are you saying exactly?"

Dr. Rhen looked at Daniel as if he didn't understand English. She looked at the clock. It was 5:02 PM. "What I mean, sir, is that by 6:00, you will be a father."

Word spread through the staff that the woman who had stayed pregnant was finally about to give birth. Delayed with another patient, Jerry ran into the room. He took Daniel's elbow gently. "They won't let you be with her when they give her the spinal block. And trust me, it ain't something you wanna see anyway. I'll get you scrubbed in and you can meet her in the OR."

Macy looked fearfully at Daniel as he helplessly shrugged his shoulders. The two were dumbfounded at the urgency of the situation. In all the weeks they had spent there preparing for this moment, they were utterly adrift at the mercy of the professionals.

A person in scrubs asked Macy to sign several forms before starting an IV. "This one says it's okay for residents and students to assist in the birth; this one says you won't sue us if the spinal block paralyzes you for the rest of your life…." He continued in a lackadaisical nature, indicating his monotony in reciting this procedure. His tone was both comforting and alarming to Macy.

Macy was bustled into the operating room. A sheet obstructed her view to her stomach. There was a pervasive smell of latex in the cold steel room. Macy was instructed to lean over for the spinal block as a long needle was inserted into the base of her spine. She was immediately strapped to a table as if it were a crucifix.

In moments, Daniel joined her at the top of the table. A sheet protected him from seeing the operation.

The first incision was made. Macy asked Daniel what was going on. He peeked over the sheet and saw Macy's intestines pulled out of her and resting on the cold metal table beside her body. He paled. Within seconds, Macy felt an incredible amount of pressure rocking her body side to side.

Daniel was patting Macy's head when she asked him to stop. Daniel froze. "Are you okay?"

Macy closed her eyes and took a deep breath. The humming of the lights seemed to mute in Macy's ears. On the next breath, her shoulders lowered away from her ears and relaxed. She closed her eyes and smelled that familiar scent that conjured up thoughts of home. Peace fell over Macy like a blanket.

Macy opened her eyes and looked at Daniel. "It's all going to be okay, Daniel. I just have this amazing peace. Our son is going to be okay. I know his name."

Moments later Dr. Rhen announced she had pulled their baby boy out of Macy's womb and now the rest would be up to the NICU staff.

There was no cry. Despite Macy's and Daniel's questions, the staff would not confirm if the baby boy was breathing or not. Macy insisted Daniel go to see their son. Daniel left her to be with their child.

Several long moments later, Dr. Rhen explained that she was stapling Macy's incision. Macy lay there relishing her epiphany. People started fading away and Macy closed her eyes again. When she opened them, Daniel was there.

"He weighs one pound, fifteen ounces. He's tiny. I mean, he looks like a baby, 'cept he's the length of a banana. He has a little hair on his back like a Chihuahua." His nervous energy made him speak fast.

Macy just listened. She felt a serenity wash over her body. She couldn't speak. She just stayed with the knowledge for a moment. When she finally did speak, she said, "Daniel, the baby is going to be okay. I just know it. I have this sense of certainty about it. Remind me of this later. It may get harder before it gets easier, but he will be okay. I just know it."

Dr. Rhen finished stitching and stapling the incision. Macy was wheeled to a recovery area and given morphine for her pain. Met by her parents and brothers in the recovery room, Macy was given a button to push that would deliver morphine, but all she wanted was an update on her son.

Oona and Carl did what they could to find out minute-by-minute updates, but hours later they didn't know anything. In an effort to distract her, her brother said, "You've gotta tell us what you decided to name the baby."

Daniel came back to the room; he was pale. He had been to see the baby and receive the latest update.

The baby was alive but on life support. It appeared he was not doing well. He was too little. Daniel looked at the room of people and proceeded to give what sounded like a eulogy on the baby's status. "It's not looking good for the baby—"

"Phoenix," Macy blurted out. "His name is Phoenix and he will rise up to his name."

As if under a spell, she dropped out of consciousness as soon as the words left her mouth. She felt like she had slept for hours but it had only been forty-five minutes when the pain woke her up. She had a catheter inside her urethra and the bag was almost full of urine. Her brothers were gone and now Macy's parents were the only ones there. Oona was softly caressing Macy's hand and Carl was holding a cool cloth to her head. Once again she was angry with herself for getting in a car accident and causing this whole situation.

The NICU doctor tapped on the door and entered the room with Daniel and Jerry behind him.

"Hi Mrs. Westcott, I'm Dr. Clark." He spoke slowly and softly. "Macy, your son did not respond well to the traditional means of life support. Since he was in a dry sac, he never had the opportunity to practice breathing. That's one of the benefits of the amniotic fluid—it allows babies to practice inhaling and exhaling. So, we had to take a different approach and put him on a more aggressive life support machine. We try not to do this because it causes the baby's body to shake, which can cause other problems, but we really didn't have any other choice. During the transition, we lost his heartbeat for about thirty seconds. I think you should prepare yourself. I'm sorry to say it, but his chances of surviving the night are fifty-fifty."

Macy heard the words like a Chinese sitcom where the voice was dubbed in too late. The doctor's words were slow and deep. They didn't match his mouth's movements. She was unable to comprehend what he was saying.

She pressed the morphine button as many times as she could and passed out. The next several hours were much of the same thing. She remembered Jerry coming in and saying, "No news is good news."

10

Macy's recovery room was in a different area of the hospital with nurses she didn't know. A few hours after the conversation with Dr. Clark, Macy woke up prepared for battle. She pulled the probes from her body and yanked the IV from her arm. Daniel was asleep on an even smaller cot in her room. She sat up in her bed, winced in pain but ignored it. She tried to stand but she could not feel her legs and the catheter felt like it was pulling her insides out. She started making demands. "Daniel, wake up! Go to the NICU and get a full report on how Phoenix is doing."

Daniel protested groggily, "Macy, it's 4:00 in the morning. They are doing everything they can. We need to give him time. Let's give it until daylight."

Macy cut him off. "Daniel, I need you to find out what exactly they are doing. I need to know. Either you can be my eyes and ears or I can find a way to get to my son. I haven't even gotten to see him, Daniel! Please do this for me." Macy's voice got louder as she pleaded with her husband.

One of the nurses came to the door. "Is everything okay in here?"

Macy took advantage of seeing a nurse. "I need to get my milk to come in so I can feed my son and keep my supply. I need you to get a pump for me. Can you do that?"

The nurse looked at Daniel, then back at Macy, then back at Daniel. Daniel was stunned at all the demands. The nurse stood blinking.

"I'll have to ask the doctor in the morning," the nurse said. "Why don't you just try and get some rest."

Macy started to object but the nurse interrupted her with a soft voice.

"Ma'am, if your baby doesn't make it, you don't want to have to deal with your milk supply being your constant reminder."

Macy shot back, "My baby is a boy. His name is Phoenix. He is not going to die, so I think it would be great if I could feed him." The more Macy spoke, the more determined she became. "So, if you don't mind getting me a pump now, I would really like to invite my supply of milk to come into my breasts." Her sentence ended with a hint of sarcasm and certainty.

The nurse continued to argue. "Ma'am, you were only six months pregnant; your mammary glands may not even be able to produce milk."

The nurse's comment was enough to fuel Macy's fire. She was furious; she wished the same staff that was in charge of her before she gave birth was still in charge. Post delivery landed her on another floor and a different wing of the hospital. She yelled toward the door and pushed the nurses' station intercom button. A voice came on the intercom.

Macy yelled, "Hi, my name is Macy Westcott. I gave birth tonight, I know my body, and I would like the opportunity to pump my milk so I can feed my baby please. Can you get me a pump?!"

The voice over the intercom responded, "We'll see what we can do."

"Thank you!" Macy yelled.

Daniel and the nurse blinked at each other and at Macy.

"Daniel, can you help them find a pump on your way to the NICU please. Thanks," she said without waiting for a response.

Daniel was stunned to see his wife behaving like a drill sergeant. He had never seen Macy act this way. Macy didn't know where it was coming from; all she knew was that her son was on life support in the NICU. Mother bear had entered stage left.

Jerry worked in the maternity ward so he wasn't around much now that Macy was recovering from surgery. Daniel decided it was time to ask for help. He called Jerry's cell. Within the hour, Jerry arranged for a lactation consultant to visit Macy. A woman in her fifties wheeled a machine next to Macy.

"Hi! I'm Lilly. I heard you put on one heck of a fight to get this pump. I'm going to help you get your milk to come in." Her voice was soothing. She was clearly someone's mother and Macy instantly liked her. She looked at Lilly, who was holding two funnels in her hand along with some kind of ointment that looked like Vaseline.

Macy let down her guard and tears filled up in her eyes. She was planning to breastfeed the baby, but she didn't know anything about this machine. "Is it even possible for me to have milk this soon?"

Lilly answered as she handed Macy a tissue, "Well, did you get pregnant?"

"Yes," Macy answered hesitantly, wondering if that was a trick question.

"Did you manage to keep that baby inside of your womb in a dry amniotic sac for about a month?"

Macy laughed and smiled, "Yes, but it's my fault—"

"Macy, it seems to me that anything's possible." Lilly gave Macy instructions on how to use the pump. "It might not come the first try, but we can keep at it. Try not to get frustrated. I have found that women respond best when they are calm. I will put a sign on the door to ensure your privacy. Maybe you can turn off the lights. Here's my personal MP3 player loaded with meditation music."

Macy was teary and grateful. "Do you think I'm delusional to try to bring in my supply even though the doctors think my son will die?"

Macy's desperate question made Lilly offer a sweet reassuring smile. "Honey, I think I'd be doing exactly the same thing you are right now. This is your initiation into motherhood. Now you know what it feels like to be a mom. You will do anything for your child."

That was exactly what Macy needed to hear. "Thank you." Finally, Macy felt the tension melt away because someone finally understood her need to do something to help Phoenix.

Lilly's voice trailed off as Macy put one of the funnels to her nipples. Lilly gave her more instructions on how to work the device then she stopped.

"I should warn you, it's a strange sensation at first. I'll give you some privacy."

Lilly disappeared out the door and Macy turned off her light and put the headphones over her ears. She secured both funnels around her nipples. The machine hummed and created a suction, alternating right and then left. It tugged Macy's nipples toward the funnel.

"Holy shit!" Macy was surprised at the force. Determined, she held the funnels in place. She felt a cramping in her uterus. Looking down through the plastic funnels, Macy felt like a cow whose udders were being manipulated into a cone shape. So far, Macy didn't see any milk. She closed her eyes and listened to the music. An image of a baby boy formed in her mind. Her breathing deepened as the image became clearer. Macy slowly went to the state of consciousness that lies between sleep and meditation. She pictured herself holding her son close to her mouth, kissing him all over his face, smelling him. Her shoulders relaxed. A fragrance began to materialize. She could smell her tapestry. That familiar scent permeated the room. She felt someone's presence and opened her eyes with a soft gaze to Lilly standing at the door. Macy drowsily became more aware of her.

Lilly leaned against the wall with a smile and whispered, "Congratulations, Mom."

Macy tilted her head. She didn't understand why Lilly was looking at her so proudly. Macy looked down at the funnels and saw beads of milk dripping off her areolas and into the funnel. It was collecting breast milk into a glass bottle that was now a quarter of the way full. Macy shook off the meditation and was fully alert now as she looked down. She didn't feel the milk coming out. She took a breath and smiled. Tears slid out of her eyes.

"Thank you, Lilly!" She laughed and cried at the same time.

Lilly said quietly, "That's the colostrum. I call it liquid gold. It has the antibodies and tons of protein Phoenix is going to need. I wasn't going to tell you, but I've never worked with a woman whose mammary glands could produce milk this early. This is amazing for twenty-six weeks."

Macy felt shy, silly, and confident. "I am a lactating gladiator! I'm a GLACTATOR!"

Both women fell into laughter. It was the first time Macy laughed since the car accident.

"Here's my card if you have any questions." Lilly put her card on Macy's meal tray and slipped out the door again.

Moments later Daniel walked into her room. He looked amused and confused. "What in God's name are those things on your tits and how are they contorting your nipples to look like that? Is that milk?"

"It's a pump for my cow udders and yes, it's colostrum. Nectar for the gods."

"Well, do you want to hear about your son?"

Macy almost dropped the pump hearing the word *son*. She sat up, ready to listen.

"Phoenix is intubated but stable. The doctors will be looking for brain bleeds, vision problems due to lack of oxygen, holes in the heart. If he remains stable for twenty-four hours, they can switch to the other life support machine."

Macy was relieved. All the information made her dizzy. She thanked Daniel and apologized for being so demanding.

"When can I see him? He's two and a half days old and I've never seen him."

Daniel was resistant but had learned his lesson. He sighed. "Okay. I'll see if we can get you a wheelchair ride to the NICU so you can see your son." Macy exhaled for a long time as she finished pumping.

It took several hours and doctors to approve it, but with Jerry's help, arrangements were finally made for Macy to go to the NICU. Dr. Clark was off now and another doctor greeted Macy and Daniel. Jerry pushed Macy's wheelchair into Section F Isolette #3.

Macy rolled up so that her face was eye level with the doors of an incubator. A handwritten card was taped to the outside of a capsule that read *Phoenix Westcott*. He was the most beautiful thing Macy had ever seen. He was perfect. Ten fingers and toes. Cords and tubing ran from him to various machines and monitors. His tiny body was bruised. He lay like a bag of bones covered in skin, but he had life in him. The doctor explained that the isolette was kept at a warmer temperature and the doors needed to stay closed. There were little armholes available as opposed to opening the entire door. Tape stretched across his face to hold a tube in place. His eyes were covered with big goggles made of foam.

The doctor asked for Daniel's wedding band. He reached through the hole and slipped Daniel's ring onto Phoenix's foot. The wedding band slipped up Phoenix's entire foot, around his ankle, up over his knee, and up his thigh. Macy and Daniel were stunned at this perspective. The doctor removed the band and gave it back to Daniel. One of the monitors chimed. The doctor assured Macy it was normal, but encouraged her to go back to her room. Macy was too weak to argue.

Oona and Carl waited outside the NICU. Carl pushed Macy back to her room.

11

"Oh, you fill my head with pieces
Of a song I can't get out.
Can I be close to you?"
— The Paper Kites

Macy was supposed to be discharged the next day. After having been a resident in the hospital for over a month now, Macy was ready to sleep in her own bed and she missed Mukha. She had bedsores and was in a lot of pain. Her vagina was starting to swell so that she couldn't close her legs well. She hesitated to sign the release forms from the hospital. It didn't feel natural to leave without her baby. She assumed the sharp pains were a common post-delivery side effect. Being in her own house to recover from the cesarean would be better. There was no choice to stay, anyway. Their insurance wouldn't pay any longer. They were kicking her out. Still, she was hesitant to leave—part of her heart was beating outside of her body now. To walk away from it felt like she would not be able to draw another breath.

Two days later, Macy's swelling vagina had become so distended she could no longer bring her legs parallel. "I don't think this is normal, Macy," Daniel said, standing back, looking at her. Her whole body shook as she tried to urinate. Daniel called her regular OBGYN and got her an appointment immediately. By the time they arrived, Macy was so weak, she couldn't walk. Her fever had spiked to 104. Daniel carried her into the waiting room. After one quick look, the ambulance was called.

"Probably an overzealous resident assisting in the delivery," her gynecologist said. He was a nice elderly man who had been delivering babies for thirty-two years. He was unable to assist with Phoenix's birth because it was too high risk. "She may need plastic surgery for that scar. The infection has tunneled over. It's not going to heal properly. We can help you arrange for home health to come to your house when she gets home. She's going to need to learn how to properly pack the site with gauze." He stated that in thirty-two years of practice he had never seen an infection like this. "I'm really sorry about everything you all have gone through, Daniel." Daniel watched the ambulance pull away with his wife once again.

Macy was taken to their local hospital where it was determined that she had necrotizing fasciitis, flesh-eating bug. The doctors decided to cut the infection out of Macy's already distorted incision. She was delirious and pumped with so many drugs she didn't regain consciousness for thirty-six hours.

During that time, a collage of images, sounds, and conversations flashed in Macy's mind. At times she became so agitated, she would thrash around her bed as if she was having an epileptic seizure, but her brain wasn't misfiring. She was dreaming. The image felt like flashbacks.

There was a field of sunflowers as far as the eye could see. The sky was bluer than Macy had ever seen. She gazed into the horizon. Every stalk had a sunflower.

"Slonecznik!"

The faint voice was scarcely perceptible behind her.

"Slonecznik!"

It was louder this time. It was a man's voice. No one was there. She heard giggles in front of her. She turned back to the sea of sunflowers. The little giggle was from a small boy's voice.

"Mama się mnie znaleźć!"

She smiled and laughed lightly at his request to be found. She loved this boy with reverence. The two played hide and seek.

"Idę na pokrycie cię pocałunkami!" His head popped up over a sunflower. He hoped she would capture him and smother him with kisses. She pretended to be frightened and surprised.

"Kim jesteś?" she asked—*who are you?*

"To ja, Niko, Mama!"

* Macy's smile fell from her face. *"Mikolaja*...Niko?" Macy recognized the boy's name. Color drained from her face.

Thrashing. Drugs. Thrashing.

While she was unconscious, one of the nurses asked Daniel if his wife was fluent in another language. After Macy stabilized, Daniel asked her about it.

"You never mentioned that you took a foreign language in high school."

"I didn't," Macy stated with a shrug.

"The nurse was convinced you speak some kind of Slavic language. She said you were flailing around in your bed having a night terror and that you yelled in another language. The nurse grew up somewhere in Central Europe and recognized the dialect. She said she calmed you down by speaking to you in Ukrainian."

Once the infection was under control and her fever dropped, she was released. Macy had only the faintest of recollections.

12

"Makes me that much stronger
Makes me work a little bit harder
Makes me that much wiser
So thanks for making me a fighter."
— Christina Aguilera

Macy learned to soak gauze in sterile saline, wring it out, ball it up, and place it in her C-section wound. She used a sterile tongue to push the moist gauze all the way over so it would heal from the back to the front. Careful to leave a little tail of the material available to pull on when it was time to change it, she covered the gaping hole with surgical tape. She stopped taking the prescribed pain medication immediately so she could drive forty-five minutes every day to see Phoenix. Daniel had used his vacation and sick days while Macy was on her bed rest. He went back to work but encouraged Macy to rest and recover more. She was a bulldozer. This was a different side of Macy that Daniel did not know. It had been several weeks since she had seen her baby. She worried he would not know the sound of her voice. She was determined to go every day, and she did.

On her way to the hospital one morning, Macy took a detour. She went toward the scene of her accident. She knew she was near the Southern Inn when she saw the big magnolia trees. She pulled over and closed her eyes. She tried to remember the woman she saw. The image came back: a woman with long red hair like Macy's running in the middle of the street in a nightgown and no shoes. Macy's heart sped as she tried to remember what happened next. She couldn't remember anything else. She instinctively placed her fingertips on the healed gash over her eye, took a breath, and drove to see Phoenix.

Each day Macy got up at 6:00 AM. She was the first mother in the NICU as soon as visiting hours began. She sat by Phoenix's isolette with her hand through the hole and sang to him. The only time she let go of Phoenix's finger was to pump milk. Eventually a tube was inserted through his belly button and fed him all of her nutrients.

Every day Macy asked if she could hold Phoenix, but he had been too unstable. Finally, the day came that Macy was going to hold her son for the first time. He weighed two pounds, four ounces. She called Daniel at work.

"They're going to let me hold him! I just went to the bathroom to pee and check my gauze. Nothing will interrupt us! I can't believe I'm finally going to hold him. I took off my bra so I can do the kangaroo thing they told us about. I wish you were here."

Daniel was thrilled. He wanted to be there to take pictures and be a part of this magical moment. He knew one thing about Macy when he met her: Despite how free-spirited and untamable she might seem, she was fantastic with children. She was going to be an amazing mother.

The nurses had a protocol for retrieving babies from the isolette. It was a delicate procedure because of the wires, probes, and equipment. Macy sat in the plastic chair eagerly waiting to hold her baby for the first time. She watched the nurse deliberately take her time transferring Phoenix to Macy. Macy's hospital gown was open in the front. Her breast was exposed, waiting to hold her baby on her chest.

The nurse gingerly laid Phoenix on Macy's chest. Tears rolled from Macy's eyes and splashed on his head. His diaper was a large Band Aid. His bare skin was against her naked chest. Finally, the two were connected again.

Macy sat in that chair singing, reading, and kissing him until visiting hours were over. She watched his monitors and listened to their beeps to make sure he was okay. She was amazed at the feeling of his skin on hers. He was the most beautiful creature she had ever seen. Jerry stopped by and took pictures and arranged for Macy to get extra visiting time.

Once the kangaroo care began, mother and son healed much more quickly than anyone anticipated. Macy was amazed at the healing power of touch. Within two months Phoenix passed the eye exam, closed the hole in his heart without surgery, and no longer required extra oxygen. Macy's wound was healing as a large jagged disfigurement. The insurance would pay for plastic surgery to repair the damage, but Macy embraced the scar as a battle wound.

There was talk about moving Phoenix to the hospital ten minutes away from Macy's home. Macy was thrilled. She would be able to see him both day and night, and started to have hope that these days would soon be behind them.

Macy arrived at the hospital just in time for visiting hours each day. She had become friendly with the nursing staff members, who acted as Phoenix's surrogates in her absence. They spent as much time with him as she did. She had grown especially fond of Jerry. Even though he was assigned to the maternity ward, he stopped by to visit her each day in the NICU. Macy asked a nurse to put Phoenix back in his isolette so she could call Daniel about the transfer. The procedure was always the same: First, the nurse opened the big door to the isolette, a rush of warm air would escape; then the nurse would weave her hand through the wires and systematically transfer the baby to the incubator.

This time the nurse began the process of shifting Phoenix back, but Macy realized she wasn't following the normal procedure. The nurse was moving more quickly than she usually did. She had retrieved Phoenix from Macy but the isolette door was still closed. The nurse realized her mistake and tried to open the heavy door while holding the baby in one arm.

It happened in slow motion as Macy started to protest. The nurse lost control of the door and dropped Phoenix from her grasp. Macy instinctively lunged, thrusting her hands to catch her son from smacking to the ground. Her hand arrived under his head just in time to cushion the impact. She dropped to her knees and hastily clutched him, folding him safely into her chest.

"Oh. My. God." Macy was afraid to pull Phoenix away from her breasts. She didn't know what she was going to see.

He wasn't crying. There was no blood. The nurse blinked and looked stunned. She couldn't believe the mistake she had just made—or that Macy was now screaming at her.

"Go get the doctors!" Macy screeched. "We need a head scan to see if he has internal bleeding. GO!" Macy barked.

The nurse was frozen in shock. Macy clutched the four-pound child to her chest. She flung the curtain open. "I need a doctor! Help!" she screamed.

Within seconds, a team of doctors rushed in to examine Phoenix. The monitors were beeping. Macy refused to put Phoenix down; she wanted to run out of the hospital with her son. She was sobbing and rocking Phoenix when Jerry arrived.

One of the NICU doctors approached Macy. "Mrs. Westcott, you've watched little Phoenix fight for his life over these last couple of months and now a human error may have caused a setback. I understand you're scared and emotional. You have every right to be. The nurse is very upset. She has dismissed herself from the NICU floor and we will take disciplinary actions. We need to examine Phoenix and see if he's okay. Can you let me do that? Jerry will stay with you." The doctor spoke to Macy like she was in a mental ward.

Macy agreed for the doctors to do a head scan but only if she could stand right next to him and not let go of his hand. They wheeled a sonogram machine over to Phoenix and applied jelly to his head. It was the first time Macy ever heard Phoenix cry. It sounded like a cat meowing.

The area cleared out while the sonogram tech did the scan. Macy kept looking at the screen. She didn't know what the fluids were and what the images flashing on the screen meant. She questioned the tech, who wouldn't tell Macy anything directly. The technician had been given orders to show the results to the doctor and the doctor would tell Macy the news.

"It may be a half hour before the doctor is able to meet with you. Why don't you go take a break?" Jerry encouraged.

Macy's eyes were puffy from crying. She was still tearing up and Daniel had no idea what had happened.

Macy ignored protocol to put regular clothes on and wash out of the NICU. She exited as quickly as she could and went to a lobby phone. She replayed the incident in her head over and over. She called Daniel at work, trying to swallow her sobs.

"Daniel. Something terrible has happened." She launched into the details, retelling the story between hiccups and gasps for air.

Daniel quietly listened. When Macy was finished, he simply said, "Well, I'm not sure I could do anything more than what you've done. What do you want me to do? If you think I should come there, I will, but it sounds like you've done everything you can, right?"

Macy was flabbergasted at Daniel's response. She understood that he had not seen the accident for himself, but how could he not understand the severity of the situation? How could he be so calm? She wanted him to come blazing up in the NICU and demand the result for the head scan right now and maybe request additional tests. Her stomach boiled and her face turned red.

"I don't want you to come because I'm asking you to, I want you to come because you're the goddamn father of our baby who was just dropped to the floor."

The phone was silent. Macy heard him take a deep breath and mutter something about "postpartum hormones."

She'd had enough. Macy stared straight ahead and simply dropped the phone to the floor and walked back into the NICU. She passed the washing station and did what she thought a man should do—she demanded results.

In that moment she became the single advocate for Phoenix's well being. All the decisions from here on would come through her. She would be Phoenix's voice. When Macy put her mind to something, even she was surprised at her own strength. Macy realized her love for Phoenix was unparalleled to anything she'd ever experienced. From this moment on, she would be his champion.

Macy was assertive, calm, strong, well spoken, straightforward, and took control back. She demanded results from the head scan and she ordered x-rays and a second opinion from an outside hospital not associated with UNC. She met with the night shift and briefed them on Phoenix's condition. She didn't ask for permission; she explained that they would be breaking their rules for the evening because she wasn't going to leave Phoenix's side. She explained if they wanted to escort her out, she would be taking her baby with her straight to the local news station and the hospital would receive the worst press they've ever gotten.

Macy met with the doctors in a conference room off the side of the NICU. They explained that there was a little swelling of cerebral tissues of the brain but there was no bleeding. They didn't feel another scan was necessary, but on Macy's insistence, they reluctantly agreed to conduct one more. Macy negotiated the next couple hours of Phoenix's care with the doctors in charge. This time, she would be allowed to hold him while he was being scanned. She also demanded that she be allowed to warm the jelly before they pasted his head with it.

Macy was relieved at the results and pleased with her newfound confidence at being Phoenix's voice. Jerry brought Macy a more comfortable chair and some blankets. She was there to stay. She asked Jerry to call Daniel and inform him she wouldn't be coming home. Once Phoenix was back on her chest, their breathing became one of a steady rhythm.

Her fears began to dissipate when suddenly Phoenix started moving his head. He lifted his head off her chest and opened his eyes. Phoenix used his strength to move his head around Macy's chest. He was hunting for something. Macy didn't know what he was doing.

"Oh God, is he having a seizure?" Macy yelled for Jerry, who rushed over and saw what was happening.

Macy became alarmed. "Is he okay?"

Jerry laughed, "Girlfriend, he's doing exactly what he's supposed to be doing. He's rooting around for your milk!" Macy let out a huge sigh and laughed. They both watched in awe.

"He's going to be hard-headed like his mom," Jerry said.

Macy rolled her eyes at Jerry, grateful for a lighthearted moment. They watched in amazement as Phoenix's natural instincts led him to her breasts.

Jerry made a puking sound. "See, that right there is why I'm gay." He pointed at Macy's breast that was leaking milk. "Not hot!" he sang.

Macy giggled at Jerry's joke. Phoenix's head had made it to her breast. His lips poked out and his breathing increased. His mouth landed on Macy's nipple. Macy had no idea what it would feel like to nurse. She had only pumped. She was thrilled with anticipation.

"The trick will be to see if he can suck, swallow, and breathe without his oxygen level dipping," Jerry whispered as if watching a doe stand for the first time.

The two watched Phoenix carefully as he latched on. They exchanged glances at the machines and at Phoenix. Macy found herself tensing up waiting for a machine to alarm but instead remembered Lilly's words about staying relaxed.

"You're doing great, Mom. Just relax," Jerry whispered and patted Macy's shoulder. "I'll give you some privacy."

Macy felt empowered at the ability to provide Phoenix with the thing that could help him sustain life and grow. She was doing it—she was providing Phoenix his life source. She was a breastfeeding mother.

Phoenix was transferred to the local hospital. Macy was with Phoenix even more. After three more weeks, he passed the tests to be discharged from the hospital. Macy's infection healed and Phoenix gained weight and strength more rapidly than the doctors predicted.

Macy embraced a life of new normalcy. She shifted into the role of full-time wife, mother, laundress, cook, and housekeeper with ease. Daniel took control of the finances and Macy handled the day-to-day activities. They finally felt like a normal family.

13

"You can't make your heart feel
Something it won't."
– Bonnie Raitt

Macy was slowly building her core strength back. She began teaching yoga again but didn't return to the gymnastic job because of the cost of childcare. Other than playing guitar and singing for Phoenix, she had not performed in a long time. Daniel had been employed at the software developing firm for several years now. He had established a decent reputation. He had spearheaded a new concept that allowed video games to be used on smaller devices like cell phones. He had great work ethic and pushed himself to keep raising the bar.

Daniel's desire to be number one in his company made him moody. The only time Macy saw him smile was at night when he read books to Phoenix. He read out loud with lively expressions and colorful voices. He doted on Phoenix in the bath. "Who is the cutest baby in the world? You are!" Work consumed the remaining hours of the day. His role as developer was overlapping with the sales and marketing departments more than he enjoyed. He was constantly checking emails, on conference calls, or locked up in his office. He wondered aloud about other jobs.

Macy often encouraged him to get a job doing something he had a passion for. "What if you become a basketball coach?"

Daniel snorted, "We'd have to sell this house and move to a one-bedroom apartment."

"Well, maybe we'd be happier if you were doing something you truly enjoyed. Let's talk about what makes you excited to get up in the morning."

Daniel was resistant. "Not everyone has a thing like you do, Macy. Not everyone needs to feel excited about what they do every day. Some people just punch the clock for a paycheck. I don't need deep conversation about philosophy and I don't want to discuss the latest Wayne Dyer book. Not everyone needs a soul revolution, Macy. And even if I did, I live in the real world where there are bills to pay." His tone was condescending.

Macy felt stifled. "Well, how about feeling inspired? You aren't even inspired to get out of your PJs when you work from home. Most days you haven't showered or brushed your teeth by lunchtime. You're so smart and creative, Daniel. I just want you to do something that makes you fulfilled. Maybe it could start as a hobby and grow into something more fruitful. I'm not asking you to go on a silent retreat. I know that's my kind of thing. But I want you to grow and evolve within your interests too. You're such a great father. Don't you want to have another child?"

In a rare moment of insecurity, Daniel admitted, "I'm not really good at this whole fatherhood thing, Macy. I'm done with kids. Haven't we been through enough? Your role is more important than mine anyway. Boys need their moms. Besides, I still don't know what I want to be when I grow up."

Macy looked at him. She thought she saw emotion welling up in his eyes.

"Maybe if I didn't have responsibilities." Daniel coughed, rolled his eyes, and went back to his office.

Daniel fell into a depression until he came up with the idea of having an extravagant birthday party for Phoenix. Macy discouraged him. "Let's just do a family barbeque and invite some of the hospital staff to celebrate?" she suggested.

Daniel began to plan the birthday party like it was his full time event-staging job. He interviewed DJs, outlined the schedule of events, and hired a magician, a caterer, and someone to do an ice sculpture.

"I think we should save the money for a birthday Phoenix will actually remember, Daniel. This is getting a little excessive, don't you think?"

"Come on Mace, it's his first birthday. Everything has been so serious. He's going to be okay, let's celebrate a little."

When he put it that way, Macy relaxed into the idea of a large-scale affair. Daniel reserved the country club in his parents' neighborhood. Macy joked that the birthday party was grander than their wedding reception.

Pat came from San Diego just for the event. After a sit-down dinner and watching Phoenix eat his first bite of birthday cake, Daniel arranged for the DJ to start the adult party. Pat and Daniel took a couple of shots of whiskey together and pulled people out to the dance floor. Macy worried that the music was too loud for Phoenix's ears. Macy decided to take him back to Mr. and Mrs. Westcott's house a block away. Daniel kissed Phoenix goodnight and kept dancing. Oona stopped Macy on the way out.

"Honey, I'll take Phoenix back to the house; you go enjoy the party with Daniel."

"Thanks anyway, Mom, but I'm tired and I'd rather just rock him to bed myself."

"I understand, honey. I never missed an opportunity to rock you either," Oona said as she walked out with her daughter and grandson.

Carl joined them in the parking lot. "You ready to call it a night, babe?" he asked Oona.

"I want one last dance with my husband."

Carl wrapped his hand around Oona's waist and the two slow danced in the parking lot.

"I might puke," Macy joked as she strapped Phoenix into his stroller. "Your Grammy and Pop-Pop are like a couple of teenagers, Phoenix."

The weeks following Phoenix's party, Daniel started sleeping a lot. He worked in his home office in his PJs until

2:00 or 3:00 without brushing his teeth. Macy heard him on the phone during conference calls. He seemed more combative than she ever remembered. He didn't stop long for lunch and drank coffee until mid afternoon. Daniel didn't enjoy his colleagues. He referred to the engineers as geeks and nerds. He had a TV connected to a gaming device and kept a little dorm refrigerator in his office stocked with beer and grey Goose Vodka. At 4:00 PM each day she heard him mixing a martini or cracking a beer open.

"Daniel, I think you're depressed, babe," she said. "You need to do what makes you happy. We can make adjustments to our lifestyle. Let's create a budget together."

"Let's see if you feel that way when you have to get a real job or when we have to pay for your next continuing education class," he shot back.

Macy tried again. "I want us to sit down and talk about finances, honey. We're on the same team. Maybe we can outline a budget and you can find a job that makes you happy."

"What do you know about budgets, Macy?" He laughed sarcastically.

The couple grew more tumultuous. He played video games and traveled more frequently. Macy eventually grew to relish her autonomy and enjoy the long stretches he was gone.

When Phoenix was three, they decided to enroll him in a half-day preschool program. Macy was able to teach more yoga classes with her flexible morning schedule now. The extra money was helpful but Daniel didn't seem to feel comforted by it.

Daniel lived under the constant supervision and critique of his boss. "She reminds me of my mother," he said. "Nothing is ever good enough." Their relationship was volatile.

His supervisor placed pressure on Daniel to meet tight deadlines and quotas. When he failed, she ridiculed him in front of his team. Macy had never seen him under so much stress. He closed himself in his office and played video games into the evening. At dinner he ranted about his loathing for corporate America while constantly checking his email on his tablet.

Macy asked Daniel to show her how to manage their checking account now that banking was available online. Daniel acted like the process was too complicated for her to understand and feigned that he didn't remember the passwords. Occasionally Macy checked their home computer for the history to see what sites Daniel was visiting. She felt ashamed for looking, but deep down, she knew he had so many devices now; he could use any of them to look at anything he wanted.

Most nights, Macy could be found on the floor playing with Phoenix in her comfortable faded orange sweatpants. Daniel called them her pumpkin pants when they first married. One night, Daniel was packing for a business trip and she mentioned how much she missed playing at gigs. She knew the money from performing would help. When she suggested it, Daniel discouraged her. "Macy, you're not a kid anymore. Are you going to bring Phoenix to the bars? I travel all the time now." He slid his tablet and zipped his suitcase as if to say "case closed."

The next morning, Macy took her magnifying mirror close to her face. Her eyes were puffy, she had several wrinkles across her forehead, and now she had crow's feet. She went to the window for natural light. She couldn't believe what she saw. There was darker hair along the edges of her lips. The copper hair around her temples showed gray. She pulled down her pumpkin pants and examined her waist, squeezing her middle. Things were softer than ever. "When the hell did that happen?"

Macy left the house at 7:00 each morning to take Phoenix to school. She would come back home after her first yoga class, walk Mukha, and go back out to teach a second and third yoga class. When Daniel was home, she didn't see him until dinnertime. He slept until 9:00, went straight into his office and usually didn't come out until after several beers or a couple of martinis in the late afternoon.

Macy thought about having another child more and more. She didn't want too much age distance between Phoenix and a sibling.

One afternoon, Macy dressed in a new bra and panties. She looked at herself in the mirror. She sucked in her stomach. She was happy to see that if she stood just the right way and did not breathe, her belly was almost flat. Her boobs took up every bit of the cup. The push-up bra made them appear like they were perkier than they actually were. That made her giddy as she danced in the full-length mirror. She thrust her hips side to side, arched her back, then stuck her chest out. It had been a long time since she felt sexy. Her belly jiggled a little so she put strands of her long hair between her cleavage, attempting to cover her stomach. She missed her dreadlocks. She turned to the side, stopped, and got closer to the mirror.

"Shit!" she said as she backed up to the mirror. It was cellulite on the side of her thigh. She smacked her leg and tried to bring a strawberry tint to the surface. *Maybe the blush color will hide the dimples.* She put the mirror back on the counter and leaned forward. Shuffling her hair around, she tried to create a new part where the gray was less obvious. Glancing over a shoulder, she sucked in her tummy and walked out.

Macy thought about the things she said in her yoga classes about self-acceptance. Now she felt like a hypocrite as she calculated her flaws. She yearned to be reassured. She lit candles, strategically placing them around the bed to hide her imperfections. Although Daniel was only in the home office, she thought it would be sexier to call him on his cell phone.

"What's up," he answered gruffly.

"Hi. I'm laying on our bed and thought you would be interested in seeing my new bra and panties?"

"Great, I just finished paying off the credit card bill. How much did that cost?"

Macy was silent.

Daniel took a deep breath. "Sorry, it's the end of the quarter, you know how stressful this time of year is."

Resisting the urge to feel disappointed, Macy pressed on. "Well, I think you should come relieve some of that stress."

Daniel sighed heavily in the phone and hung up. Macy could tell by his distracted tone he wasn't coming. She was disappointed. What man refused sex? Especially a man that needs a mental break.

Macy looked at herself in the mirror. Her eyes were dim. The new underwear was a little too skimpy anyway. She flopped down on her bed and was soon joined by Mukha. He wanted to jump on her bed, but he was less agile in his older age.

"Hey buddy! You wouldn't walk away from a chance to mount your bitch, would you?" She laughed as she assisted him on the bed.

Macy lay there a few minutes, giving Mukha her undivided attention. She scratched the bedding and he dove into her hand the way he used to when it was just the two of them. The two playfully barked at each other. It was rare for Mukha to be feisty anymore.

He quickly ran out of energy. The two settled down and lay nose to nose. Macy's head chattered…she didn't remember many times that Daniel rejected her physically. He used to chase her around the kitchen and make out. Macy and Mukha snuggled in the bed until her eyes were heavy.

Macy dreamed of eagles flying in and out of canyons. They collected thorny ironwood twigs to make a nest. The eagles padded the sharp thorns with sunflowers. As the babies grew, space became limited. Food was in bigger demand. Survival became difficult. The adult eagle began to pluck away the sunflowers, exposing the thorns beneath. The babies became too uncomfortable. They eventually had to choose to live in pain or fly. A single sunflower blew in the wind, rocking east to west.

Macy woke up.

Longing to have another child, Macy often dreamed about getting pregnant again. She adored Phoenix. He would make a great big brother. The moment she got pregnant with Phoenix, she couldn't wait to do it again. She wanted to have several kids close together in age. She wanted her house to be loud and chaotic.

For months, Macy went through the motions of living. She tried to encourage Daniel, giving him pep talks. The harder she pushed, the more he withdrew. She felt discouraged and unattractive. She wore her pumpkin pants each evening and devoted her attention to Phoenix. She was stripped raw like a ligament torn from a muscle.

As Daniel's stress intensified, his control over finances grew. Macy and Phoenix went to three different grocery stores to strategically use coupons. Daniel went over the receipts and chided her for unnecessary luxuries.

Macy tried to initiate intimacy with Daniel one night and he was unable to get firm. Macy began to give up on her dream of having more children. When Daniel didn't travel for work, he played video games, watched sports TV, or stayed in his office until late in the evening. Macy realized it was lonelier with Daniel home than when he traveled. She kept busy with baths and books for Phoenix and planned for classes after she tucked him in. She made an appointment to get her gray hair colored and started running again.

Macy needed a new pair of running shoes but hated to ask Daniel about the financial situation. She asked for the password to their account. Daniel was perplexed at her interest in the account and said he didn't know the password. She asked if they could sit down and go over finances to create a budget. Daniel's typical response became, "Maybe another time." Macy's paychecks were being deposited into an account she had no control over.

Macy didn't know if they were in debt or had a surplus. She didn't like being in the dark but she didn't want to start an argument. Every time she brought up finances, Daniel became territorial. Rather than argue, Macy went to local thrift stores when she needed something. Before dropping Daniel's suits at the cleaners, Macy rummaged the pockets for loose change. One day she slid her finger into the slit of his breast pocket and found a condom. Alarmed at her discovery, Macy picked up Phoenix from preschool early and immediately went home to ask Daniel about it.

Daniel didn't expect Macy home and she overheard him on the phone. It sounded like the old Daniel. He was gregarious, his voice full of inflection. Macy was thrilled to hear happiness in his throat. She wondered who he was talking to.

He was surprised to see her home as he came down from his office. He had color in his face and seemed lighter on his feet.

"Hi! You look happy. Who were you talking to?"

"Oh, that was Jesse."

Macy had heard him refer to Jesse before. "Oh! Is there good news at work? What did he say?" Macy asked enthusiastically.

"Well, first of all, no offense, but you wouldn't understand the deal we're working on—it's complicated. And second, Jesse is not a he. Short for Jessica. She's brilliant! We're killing this deal together. By the way, I'll be traveling to Toronto several times over the next several months to manage the graphics on this new video game we're launching and she'll sweet talk the sales. We're leaving tomorrow to launch."

Macy's intuition screamed. She tried soothing herself but her head incessantly chattered. She reprimanded herself for being insecure. She should be happy he was enjoying his job. Daniel went on business trips with women all the time. His voice just seemed so different when he spoke to her.

And now the condom.

Macy followed Daniel around the house as he began packing. She and Phoenix sat on the bed next to his suitcase. "Tell Daddy how much we're going to miss him, Phoenix."

Phoenix uttered his favorite word, "No!" Phoenix was challenging every request these days. His favorite words were "no" and "why." Macy knew Phoenix was just testing the waters but neither of them liked it.

"Jesse's kid could read entire books by the time he was three. What are they doing in his preschool?" Daniel asked.

Just the mention of her name conjured up a sick feeling in Macy. "So you tell Jesse about Phoenix?"

"Sure, we spend a ton of time together, it can't be all business. She's sharp. She's a mother of two, independent saleswoman making six figures a year. She's got her shit together. I'll ask her how she potty trained her son, Maverick. Maybe she can give you some tips."

Macy felt small. Daniel started brushing his teeth.

"Her husband must be very happy." Macy was fishing for details.

"Nah, she's divorced," he answered through his toothpaste.

Macy felt sick. "Well, she sounds like the total package."

Daniel heard the sadness in her voice. He softened and spit his toothpaste out and wiped his mouth. "Hey. You two are the total package. I'll only be gone during the week. The weekend will be here before you know it." He poked Phoenix in the belly to make him laugh and turned to continue packing.

Macy pulled the condom she found in Daniel's suit. She tossed it down on the bed. "Well, I hope you won't be needing this."

The color drained from Daniel's face for a moment, then he quickly laughed. "Awe, tradeshow jokes, Macy. It was just a joke souvenir from the last tradeshow."

Two things happened the first week Daniel was gone: Macy potty trained Phoenix and she got a credit card in her own name. Macy sought refuge from her own mind. Daniel's need for control on finances left her feeling like she had to defend every purchase she made. She decided to become an individual again. The first thing she treated herself to was the rage and all over the media—it was called Botox. A lot of her yoga students had done it; they were even throwing Botox parties. It was a cutting edge way to make wrinkles disappear. So, for a few hundred dollars, she received her first Botox injection and bought skin care products.

Daniel squirmed when Macy talked about continuing education credits. In order to maintain national accreditation in yoga, she had to take an instructor-level course every year. Daniel went on about how continuing education was a racket. She had already satisfied this year's requirements, but things had been so tense between them lately, especially regarding finances, that she had no idea how she was going to satisfy next year's requirements to Daniel.

Instead of talking about it with him, she made her second purchase on her new credit card. She signed up for a teacher-training course.

14

"I've been afraid of changing
'Cause I've built my life around you."
– Fleetwood Mac

Dropping Phoenix off at preschool proved to be a challenging task every day. Macy walked him to the classroom where he wrapped his entire body around her leg.

"Pleath no go, Mommy!" he would cry with a slight lisp as his bottom lip quivered.

The teachers would help unwrap him from her leg and she would make a sad escape. The first three days of preschool, Macy cried harder than he did. Phoenix would say his head hurt. Macy always felt guilty. He would start kindergarten next year. Macy was hopeful it would be less traumatic for them both.

Most weeks, Daniel traveled Monday through Friday. Mukha started losing bladder control and Daniel suggested it was time to put him down.

"You can't just come back in town and declare him unfit to live!" Macy snapped at the suggestion. But Macy knew her dog was no longer happy.

The class Macy had signed up for was about to begin. She was thankful for the distraction from her aging pup. Class was held every Tuesday and Thursday afternoon for three months. Macy rearranged her schedule with her employer so that she would maintain the same amount of hours and pay. Since Daniel was gone so much, she didn't have to justify her whereabouts yet. Macy realized that even when Daniel was home, he probably wouldn't even notice her missing. On the weeks Daniel didn't have to travel for work, he went to visit Pat in California and visited a client there so he could write off the trip as a business expense.

The evening before her class, Macy went on her rounds to the grocery stores. She noticed how much cheaper the bill was when Daniel traveled. As she was walking down the coffee aisle, she paid close attention to how much she wasn't spending in Daniel's absence. She calculated approximately how much that was—it came close to $70. She paused when the cashier asked if she wanted any cash back. She realized she could pay for her yoga class with the money she was saving while Daniel was gone. He might not notice if she "lost" the receipts. So, Macy withdrew $70 each time she went to the grocery store, then trashed the receipt. Macy told Daniel that the yoga studio where she was employed was paying for her to receive continuing education credits and that they had offered to pay for the eight-month course.

Macy knew another child wouldn't help their marriage, but she couldn't deny her longing to give Phoenix a sibling. She rarely brought it up to Daniel anymore because it inevitably caused a fight. And at this point, she no longer wanted to have another child with him. Mukha's age was a reminder of how quickly time goes.

15

"I feel so alone on Friday nights
Can you make it feel like home?"
– Lana Del Rey

Macy pulled into the parking lot of the boutique aerial yoga studio. She was excited and nervous about expanding her practice. She needed these credits to maintain her certification but today her energy was scattered. She felt guilty for lying to Daniel about paying for this class. Mukha was not well, Phoenix wasn't happy in school, and she felt a sense of heaviness. She was coming undone.

Macy sat in her car for an extra moment, closed her eyes, and asked the universe for assistance. "Divine source of all creation, fill me with your thoughts. Allow me to accept these teachings with grace and ease. Allow me to make new connections that will serve my highest good and align me with my highest being. Help me to be all of my potential. Bring forth my guardian angels. Keep me grounded and in tune with the highest vibrations possible." Macy took a deep breath in and felt the tension melt away from her neck and shoulders.

Macy was greeted by a friendly receptionist behind the counter. She was a brown-eyed blond girl about the same age as Macy. She had a warm smile and welcoming aura. Macy instantly liked her. She led Macy up the stairs and through a set of private doors into a small studio. Macy's eyes lit up. It was a beautiful space. Turquoise sheer fabric hung from the ceiling and draped to the floor in puddles around the perimeter of the room. The ceiling was cloaked with the same flowing material, but it had been tufted to the ceiling so that it felt like blue puffy clouds surrounded her. Light spilled in the windows. A prosperous Buddha statue sat at the front of the room on an altar.

"Eight people are registered for the aerial instructor course and you're the first to arrive. Jakub will enter once everyone has arrived. The restroom is over there if you need it." She turned and left Macy alone.

The refurbished studio was on the second floor of a building in downtown Raleigh. The floors were made from old reclaimed pinewood. Macy loved to feel them creak under her feet.

Macy walked the perimeter of the room. She hummed to hear the acoustics. Her voice bounced off the walls and made her smile. She was looking forward to working with such a highly esteemed yogi. Jakub Pulaski was widely known. His Polish origin led him through Switzerland, France, Russia, and across the entirety of Europe. He came from extreme poverty. She wondered how he got into aerial yoga.

Macy picked up a bio that outlined Jakub's background. The majority of his upbringing took place in a small southern city near the border of the Czech Republic. Krakow was the central site of the Nazi general government during WWII. There is a residual solemn feeling where he grew up given it was also the home of the Plaszow Concentration Camp and the Oskar Schindler Factory. He had an impressive background traveling and training dancers and choreographers in the Cirque du Soleil. Macy knew nothing of the harrowing experiences of his childhood but the first time she looked into Jakub's eyes, she saw deep sadness.

Macy placed her mat directly in the puddle of the sunshine that cascaded through the window. She smiled at the thought of Daniel teasing her about taking a catnap in the sun. The thought of a cat made her want to start there, so she got on her knees, inhaling, arching her back, opening her chest, and exhaling to round her back like a feline.

She had a feeling she was being watched, but no one was visible. She became still and listened. She heard the receptionist downstairs.

When she finally heard other voices several minutes later, she moved to a seated lotus pose and placed the backs of her hands palms up.

16

"In your eyes
The light the heat
In your eyes
I am complete."
— Peter Gabriel

Macy's classmates started filing in one by one and she turned to greet them with a smile and "Sat nam." She quietly introduced herself. There were six women and two men.

The receptionist came in. She cleared her throat. "Ladies and gentlemen, it is with great honor I introduce you to your instructor. We are very lucky to have Jakub at our humble establishment. I will smudge each of you with sage to purge any negative energies that you may be holding on to. When everyone is clear of lower vibrations, Mr. Pulaski will join you."

The receptionist called each student one by one. With burning sage in one hand, she held the bundle over the student's head and used the other cupped hand to direct the smoke so that it surrounded their entire body. After each person was smudged, an Indian flute filled the room with a calming sound.

Macy closed her eyes and took her attention to her third eye just between her brows. She focused on the space between her breath. She saw an eye with long eyelashes. It was a vibrant indigo color. It was like nothing she had ever seen when meditating. It made her happy.

When she softened her gaze to open her eyes, Jakub Pulaski was sitting on a mat in front of the room.

17

"Call it magic, call it true
I call it magic when I'm with you
And I just got broken, broken into two
Still I call it magic, when I'm next to you."
– Coldplay

Jakub Pulaski sat quietly in front of his students. His eyes were closed. His exhale created a growling effect in the back of his throat. The class understood this to be Ujjayi breathing. The deeper his breath, the deeper the breath of his students. It was a purposeful technique he used often to energetically connect with his classes. Although he was not a large or tall man, his demeanor was powerful. He was lean, his hair mostly dark but with a distinguished amount of gray sprinkled through. His eyebrows were thick, and below them, his eyes a chestnut brown.

If taken out of context, Jakub's features would have been too big, too bold, too sharp, too slanted for his medium but defined frame. His nose was large, his nostrils wide. His eyes slanted downward, his lips were full. His forehead was flat, his bottom teeth were crooked. His chin squared sharply at the edges. However, when combined on him, the characteristics conspired to create a striking hallmark of exotic European beauty. Jakub's voice was a soft yet commanding tenor. When he smiled, his crow's feet were more pronounced, but he quickly hid his teeth with his lips.

Over the next several weeks, the yoga class became one of Macy's favorite things. It was mentally demanding, physically grueling, psychologically challenging. There were essays due, books to read, aerial techniques to choreograph, Sanskrit and anatomy to learn.

Jakub didn't accept anything less than perfection from his students. He demanded respect with his posture. He was confident, assured, and pushed without words. He observed his students closely and they wanted to deliver their best to him. He was inspiring.

Over a period of a month, the classmates became like a family. They shared everything from vegan recipes to intimate details of their lives, forming a strong bond. Jakub never shared personal information with them, but enjoyed listening to them talking among themselves. The energy in the room gave comfort to Macy. She was compelled to share things with her class that she never told anyone. She told them about her childhood church, Phoenix's birth, her frustration with Daniel, how she was struggling with her self-confidence. She and her new friends had been through the spectrum of emotions together during this course. Macy threw herself into her practice like never before.

Jakub assigned each student a major and a minor focus. They had to research and prepare a lesson for their classmates. Macy's major assignment was to learn about the Chakra system and how it can be manipulated through yoga. Her minor was to understand and articulate her understanding of each aerial inversion. Each student was responsible for creating a guided meditation based on his or her assignment. Macy's work was meticulous, precise, exhaustively detailed, and extensively organized. She included more than what was required and implemented a flawless delivery. Macy electrified the room when she delivered her lesson. The accolades went on for days. Macy grew more passionate and confident than she had been in a while.

Macy's classmates met each other out for tea or cocktails. They attended each other's classes and gave constructive criticism. Jakub was still a mystery. His English was excellent, though his accent was thick. He remained reserved and deliberate about the words he spoke.

For the final exam, Jakub explained, each student would meet with him privately. He passed around a clipboard with dates and times. Each student would deliver an exclusive aerial experience directly to him. It would include a minor focus previously presented by another student.

His slanted eyes reached for a friendly smile. "So, I hope you absorbed the information from your class members."

Macy was nervous about this final piece. She held the clipboard and selected August 13 at 7:00 PM. It was the last date possible and would give her the most time to prepare.

18

"The first time ever I saw your face
I thought the sun rose in your eyes
And the moon and the stars were the gifts you gave."
– Roberta Flack

The weeks leading up to the final exam, Macy's nerves were magnified. She spoke to some of the other students who already completed their final exam. They had all passed, but they agreed it wasn't easy.

On the evening of the exam, Macy cooked dinner for Phoenix and Daniel and left directions for reheating. Phoenix wasn't used to Macy going out at night. He didn't want her to go. He had another headache and his eyes looked tired. Daniel encouraged her, "I can handle things. Go take your exam. We'll be fine." It was the first supportive thing Daniel had uttered in weeks.

Macy arrived at the studio early the evening of her final exam. She needed to gather her meandering thoughts. She decided to meditate. She walked the perimeter of the studio, skimming her fingers along the silky hammock. She put headphones on and listened to music. She moved in an easy rhythm around the room, gently grasping and leaning away from each swing she grabbed. Her hair flowed easily as she loosened up.

She got the feeling that she wasn't alone. She stopped, unrolled her mat, and turned off her music. Macy took several deep breaths and asked her angels to guide her through the exam process. In her mind's eye, she smudged the mat and sat down in the middle. After a few moments, she settled into the lotus position. She looked, with her lids covering her vision, to the place between her eyebrows. She asked her spirit guides for a vision that would allow her to be authentic. She saw an image of a sunflower. Her hands came together, sealing at the palms in Anjali mudra. Her eyes were closed.

She wasn't sure why her lids softly started to part, but as they did, she realized Jakub was sitting inches across from her, mirroring her exactly. Even his hands were in the prayer position like hers. His eyes were closed and his breath was in the same tempo. An odd sense of relaxation came over her.

Careful not to break the silence of the room, Jakub's voice eased into the walls. He did not open his eyes.

"Shall we begin?"

Jakub informed her that her minor would be on aerial stretching with guided adjustments. She couldn't remember which of her peers had presented the anatomical section. She quickly rummaged through her brain for anatomy, kinetics, biology, muscles, fascia, and bones. She took a deep breath and pulled a few terms to the forefront of her brain.

Macy was the teacher and Jakub the student. She started, gently prompting out loud. She moved them from their seat into some familiar flows and salutations. As she moved, she gained rhythm and took control like a warrior confronting battle. Jakub followed her cues with precision. They moved in sync to her prompts. With each movement, she grew more confident and proceeded into laborious inversions assisted by the silks. They moved in perfectly synchronized moves for thirty-eight minutes. When she came to a close, they were sweltered with perspiration. The practice ended in a mandatory corpse pose, at which time Jakub moved to crack the window for fresh air.

It was dark now and cooler outside. Hearing the crickets, Macy suddenly realized she had delivered the entire presentation without music. It was part of her grade. She gasped, "My playlist! Oh no, I forgot—"

With a wave of a hand, Jakub motioned not to be concerned. "You are not finished. You may play your music during your minor presentation if you would like."

Macy quickly jumped up and placed her CD in the stereo. She had worked hard on her playlist and he didn't even know how much music meant to her. She never mentioned her passion for music in front of her classmates. How could she have forgotten it?

Jakub knew she was admonishing herself internally. He sat up. "Demolish the bridges behind you...then there is no choice but to move forward."

Macy recognized the quote.

"Let us move on, Macy." It was the first time she remembered him using her name. It sounded like a melody off his tongue. "I am the student and you are the teacher."

Macy composed herself. "We will begin by stretching the iliotibial—"

"No," Jakub interrupted softly.

"Oh. Okay." Macy was caught off guard by his quiet outburst.

"Begin again."

Macy wondered what she did wrong. She took a deep breath—then realized her mistake. It needs to start with the breath.

"Take a deep breath," she instructed.

Jakub did as directed.

"Let's begin by sweeping the leg—"

"No!" Jakub cut her off again, more firmly this time.

Now Macy was baffled. She stood numbly. "Well, what should I start with?" she asked with a rise to her tone.

"Macy, when a baby begins to move from crawling to walking, he sometimes stumbles, yes?"

Macy nodded in agreement and wondered what this had to do with anything.

"You don't shout for him to stand. You gently guide; you invite and encourage him. Yes?"

"Of course," Macy answered.

He walked a circle around Macy and stopped directly behind her. "You are thinking too much. Free your mind. You want to inspire movement, not motivate it with a forceful nature. Use energy to influence this movement. Stir the freedom of movement so it is the next organic and obvious step." He spoke with great inflection and passion. "Freedom. Unleashing the power of freedom. Do you know how to trap a monkey, Macy?"

She exhaled a nervous laughter. "No."

"You cut a cantaloupe like a…how you say…jack-o-lantern?"

Macy nodded.

"Remove the top, put a banana inside, and fasten the top back on. Instead of a face, cut a small hole into the side just big enough for monkey's wrist to fit through. Monkey comes, sees the hole and the banana. Monkey reaches for the banana. Ah, but there is a problem! Monkey cannot remove the banana. He struggles. Now he is trapped. Do you know what he has to do to be free, Macy?"

He moved in front of her. Inches of warm air was all that separated them. Their eyes met.

"Let go," they said in unison.

"Invite freedom into your practice. Let go of the way you think things should be. Let go, Macy."

He maintained eye contact with her as he threaded his fingers through each of hers, one at a time. He took his time. He drove his thumb into her palm and added gentle pressure. He decreased and added the pressure, squeezing gently all the way up to her middle finger. His movements followed her breath. He followed each finger this way, giving each one its time and attention. When he had completed each finger, he threaded it through each of his. He opened their hands that were now laced together and stretched her fingers back gently. After playing guitar all these years, she didn't realize how good the attention to these areas could feel. He was certainly intuitive.

Jakub summoned her fingers wide and pulled her arm out by her side, wrapping the silk around it. In an involuntary reflex, her head delicately dropped to the opposite shoulder. The stretch along her neck was intensely delightful. He kept his fingers laced between hers while he slid his free hand up her forearm, shoulders, neck and landed considerately on her temple. With the weight of a nickel, he tenderly invited a deeper stretch through her neck. His touch felt electrifying. Macy's heart began to race. She noticed a heat building between their hands and swallowed hard.

He wrapped the silk so it held the weight of her body. She could lean her entire weight into it, opening her side. She felt sensual. An energy current seemed to be building in the room.

Macy closed her eyes and took several slow breaths. His grip on her hand grew stronger and then weaker, as if it was a slow pulsating heartbeat. His other hand held her shoulder now. As he made his way down her arm again, she noticed that her breathing had changed slightly. Her meditative deep breaths were now faint and shallow. She could feel his eyes on her, inspecting her features. Bravely, she cracked one eye just slightly. She caught a glimpse of him in the reflection of a mirror. His eyes were closed and his eyebrows were furrowed as if he was listening with a stethoscope. He looked as though he was in pain and yet delighted at the same time. He was using her breath to lead the pulls, tugs, and tractions. She quickly closed her eyes and chided herself. He was illustrating how to give guided adjustments.

Jakub moved through the next several stretches as though leading a choreographed dance. As if in a trance, he guided her fluidly to an assisted spinal twist. Jakub swept her arm over her head. He moved toward her. The silk cradled her like a baby. His fingers were still woven between hers. Her bicep was against her ear. He gently tugged her arm so that it stretched down to her side. With his other hand, he placed the outside of his thumb on the inside of her arm and slowly slid it from the inside of her tricep to her armpit. He grazed the side of her breast down her ribs, ticking off each one, along her oblique and finally rested at her hipbone just above her waistband.

Jakub's other hand never left hers. Now he put their joined hands on her stomach. In an attempt to keep her sacrum neutral, he gently cradled her hipbone with his palm. Macy felt weak from her excelled heart rate and inability to fill her lungs completely with oxygen. No one had ever navigated her hips this way. She was overwhelmed at the intimacy of these stretches.

What happened next shocked her even more. With his fingers never unlacing themselves from hers, he began to lead their hands in circles around her belly button. He was gentle and completely in control. Now Macy knew for sure, this was unorthodox practice. This wasn't a stretching technique. This was definitely not just in her head. What was going on? Still she tried to rationalize…to dignify the arousal of her body. The movements of their hands circled her belly button several times but each time around, the circles got larger and larger. Her breathing was panting; she had to turn her head because she could feel his eyes on her.

Each time his circles got larger, she would excrete moisture from her vagina. His finger touched her C-section scar. Macy's eyes shot open. They devoured each other with their eyes—locking and not moving. Neither of them spoke or broke their gaze. It felt surreal.

Slowly, his head leaned closer and closer to her face.

Oh my God! Is he about to kiss me?

He was two inches from her face. She was completely still, watching him come closer and feeling her vagina soak her G-string. She didn't want him to come closer yet she craved for him to close the distance.

Aroma sizzled from his skin. At first Macy couldn't place it. Just as Jakub's face was less than an inch from hers, she identified the smell. It was her tapestry from India. It was the smell of a home she had never known. Macy held Jakub's gaze and watched him move in closer until his lips enveloped hers.

The kiss was unexpected. There was a magnetism between them that she had never felt before.

"Oh my God," she exhaled and quickly turned her head. "I can't do this, I'm married. What just happened?"

"I'm so sorry." He was shaking—they were both shaking. He lowered his head to rest on her shoulder. She could feel his breath and his heart racing. She assaulted him with a barrage of questions as she unwound herself from the silks.

"What just happened? When did you decide to do that? Have you ever looked at me in this way before? Have you ever done this with a student?"

He quickly lifted his head. "No, no Macy!" He was insulted. "Of course I have never done this with a student. I do not travel the world and build up my reputation this way to take advantage of women." He had a lonely pain in his eyes. He leaned away from her and looked down. "I should not have done that. It was wrong. Very wrong. Unprofessional." He was still close enough that Macy could detect that familiar scent. That distinct smell. Now it was driving her crazy. He looked bewildered and shocked by his own behavior. He harshly drove his fingers through his hair and looked away so she couldn't see the tears welling up in his eyes. They looked at each other for a minute…then for a minute more.

Jakub cleared his throat, trying to compose himself. He was obviously aroused. "Macy, I apologize. I will see to it that you are reimbursed for this course. I will tell the Board of Yoga what I have done. You will never see me again."

He turned to gather his things. This man who had seemed so certain of himself all of these months was disheveled, vulnerable, even helpless. The man she had come to admire, respect, and hold in such high esteem was now visibly shaking in front of her.

For the first time, she really looked at him. It was the first time she truly saw his face. He was stunning. It was like she had been wearing a thick veil and couldn't see what was on the other side. Suddenly the veil was pierced and she could see. She didn't know how she had never seen him this way before.

She saw him in his humanness. He was ashamed. She was overwhelmed by the impulse to reach out, grab and console him. She placed her hand over his.

"Hey, it's okay. It was a mistake. There's no need to go to such extreme measures. I'm not going to turn you in or anything. I won't speak of it again." Her nipples were at full attention through her shirt. She was completely awakened. Her vagina was more than damp; it was secreting a desire for sex.

He lifted his head slowly. Their eyes locked. Neither one moved. Once again, she saw his face.

I see your face now, a voice from the back of her mind whispered. Her eyes must have communicated her thoughts to his because he came close enough that she could feel his hungry breath against her face. In one intoxicating movement, another kiss. This time it was mutual.

Macy felt like she was having an out-of-body experience. To have another man's mouth covering her lips felt so strange to her. She felt alive and attractive. Powerful even. A sharp contrast to feeling frumpy as she often did. Millions of thoughts rampaged through her mind. *What is he thinking? Does my breath stink? Can he tell how aroused he's making me? His lips are so soft and moist. He smells like home. Who does this kind of thing to a married woman? I want more. He knows I'm married. He's heard me speak of Phoenix.*

Macy quickly pulled away from Jakub. She stared at him for a split second, shook her head as if waking up from a dream. She briskly grabbed her things and rolled up her yoga mat. She shoved it in her bag with force.

"May I please call you, Macy?" Jakub asked as he helped her gather her belongings. "I am so sorry. I need to talk to you more. I need to explain…." His voice trailed off.

"Look, I sent you a mixed message here. Sorry about that. I have a family. Please don't call me," Macy said firmly. She turned and ran down the stairs.

She fled to her car in the dark, her mind a void. She couldn't form a complete sentence in her brain. She had no recollection of the drive home, except that she pulled over at the corner one block away from the yoga center and threw up in the street.

The next thing she knew, she was sitting in her driveway.

Mukha was at the door lying in a puddle of his own urine. Macy knew it was time to put him down. Macy walked into her home to find Daniel and Phoenix on the couch.

"Hi Mommy!" they sang in unison.

A wave of guilt swept through her. Without making eye contact, Daniel turned his head so his voice was thrown over his shoulder. "How was the final exam?" He paused the game.

"Yeah, Momma. Congratulations! Did you do good on your test, Mommy? Mommy, my head hurts." Phoenix was lying with his head on Daniel's lap. Macy could see the shine of the vapor rub on his head where Daniel had rubbed Phoenix's temples.

The scene jarred her from her bewilderment, causing her to drop her keys. She bent down to retrieve them and looked at her husband and son snuggled on the couch waiting to hear about her exam. Suddenly Macy felt overwhelming affection for her family. She was angry with Jakub. How could he have been the catalyst that moved her to the point she broke her vow to her family?

"By the way, Mukha pissed in the corner. You mind getting that?" Daniel asked.

19

"I used to recognize myself
It's funny how reflections change
When we're becoming something else
I think it's time to walk away."
– James Bay

Overwhelmed with guilt, Macy felt an urge to reconnect with Daniel. He had been so busy and stressed out over the last couple of years. His beautiful blond hair was starting to recede, he had gained some weight, and Macy was concerned about his blood pressure. He got agitated with her and Phoenix easily. He considered himself to be the breadwinner of the family and the gravity of his responsibilities weighed on his mind daily.

"Daniel, I think we really need to get away," Macy began. "We need a vacation. I know we really can't afford it right now, but I have $1,000 still saved from the last few gigs I did," she lied. She was going to use her credit card to pay for it. "Can we just get the heck out of dodge for a weekend?" She pressed him with urgency.

He looked at her for the first time since she had arrived home from the exam. "Honey, Phoenix isn't feeling well, can we talk about this later?"

"Come on Daniel, this is really important to me. We need time away from Phoenix to reconnect."

"Hey, I want to come!" said little Phoenix.

"We're not going anywhere, Phoenix. Macy, it ain't gonna happen right now. I know you're blissfully unaware, but the fairy mechanic doesn't come at night to rotate your tires, top off your fluids, and change your spark plugs; you see, I just paid to have all that done."

"I just said I would pay for it."

"With what? All that money you make? Ha! In order for me to keep paying the bills, Macy, I have to stay employed. That means I actually have to go to work—I can't just take off anytime I want. I know this is foreign to you since you pretty much get to do whatever you please. Some of us actually have serious jobs that pay for important things like health insurance."

Macy felt belittled. She hated it when Daniel was condescending to her. When did he start speaking to her this way? She thought of Jakub. This time, she felt like she deserved harsh words from Daniel.

Macy tossed in bed all night. She tried every technique she knew of to go to sleep. Every time she was close to unconsciousness, Jakub's face appeared in her mind. His accent. His touch. The heat that built up between them. Macy put a pillow over her head and stuck headphones in her ears.

At 4:00 she gave up. She got up, made herself some tea, and replayed the events that took place. She sat at the kitchen table looking into her tea but seeing the images in her mind. How could she have let this happen? How could she be sitting here aroused by thinking about it? Maybe if she masturbated just once to the memory it would go away, she thought. Just once. So, sitting at the kitchen table, Macy relived the moments with Jakub.

An inordinate amount of guilt ensued as she washed her hands. She took her tea to their computer and did something she never did. She spent $987 with her credit card on a trip for her and Daniel. She opened up a browser and printed off a picture of a cruise ship and drew stick figures of herself and Daniel doing cannonballs off the pool deck.

She closed the browser and noticed a PayPal icon on the computer's desktop. She clicked on it. Thousands of dollars worth of transactions appeared. Macy scrolled through the list. She saw payments to American Express, Chase, and Visa. She was confused; she didn't understand what she was looking at. They only had one family credit card—a MasterCard. She knew Daniel would be angry with her for looking through his transactions, but something felt off about this.

She closed the browser and sat back in the seat. She was filled with determination to save her marriage. She would do more research on this later.

She made Daniel breakfast in bed and brought him the homemade brochure. "Good morning, sleepyhead. I made your favorite honeybuns for breakfast." She had a playful singsong tone to her voice. She was wearing a black spaghetti strap nightgown Daniel's mother had given her ten years ago. She put the tray on his bedside table and lightly kissed Daniel's cheeks.

"Come on honey, wake up. I have to show you something."

Daniel groaned, reluctantly sat up, and received the breakfast tray in his lap. "You know I don't feel like eating as soon as I wake up, Macy. I like to have a cup of coffee first and *then* eat."

"Yeah, yeah, yeah, that's why you have two cups of coffee on your tray."

Satisfied, Daniel picked up his mug. He used the same coffee mug religiously. Daniel looked down to see what Macy had printed off the computer. "What's this?" he asked, holding up the makeshift art.

"Well, I had an impulse to be a little crazy. Don't be mad. I booked a vacation for us."

"Jesus Christ, Macy!" Daniel set the coffee cup down so hard it spilled.

Macy jumped back to avoid being splashed by the hot beverage. She spoke quickly. "I paid for it. It was my money. You'll only have to take half a day off work. You have tons of PTO saved up—you have to use it or you'll lose it. I should have consulted you, but—"

"You're damn right you should have consulted me. What's gotten into you, Macy?" He was furious. He shoved the breakfast tray off to the side and went into the bathroom.

Two weeks later, the two were in Charleston boarding a four-day, three-night cruise to the Bahamas. Daniel was less than thrilled. She wished she had not made such a spontaneous decision. It was just creating a deeper wedge between them.

Daniel wore a scowl the first day. The two sat quietly on the pool deck watching the other couples splash each other in the diving contest. In their room, Daniel was concerned about the noise level.

"I hope we won't be able to hear this in our cabin. It's funny now, but at 3:00 AM when we're trying to sleep...."

That night as Daniel slept peacefully in a quiet room, Macy allowed her mind to revisit the experience she had in the yoga studio with Jakub. How could that have happened? How could she have allowed it to happen? She replayed every moment over in slow motion. In the freedom of her mind, she didn't leave out one moment, touch, look. She didn't realize it at first, but her breathing had changed. She was aroused beyond measure. She shut her eyes tightly. "Okay, enough!" she chided herself.

The next day, Macy and Daniel got off the boat to explore Nassau. Daniel recommended they not spend more than $10. Macy softly objected, "Come on, hon. I want to get Phoenix a couple of trinkets."

"That's the thing about vacations, Macy. It's not just the cost of the vacation...you have to factor in the cost of meals, gifts, entertainment...." He spoke to her as if she was a child. "Look at the quality of this stuff. It's crap," he said, holding up a wooden flute.

Macy's thoughts crept back to Jakub. She wondered if he was having trouble keeping his thoughts off her too. She spent time that night playing different scenarios in her mind. What if she didn't have sense enough to stop him? Would they have had sex? The thought made her embarrassed yet she couldn't help playing it in her mind. Was he imagining what she looked like naked? When did he start to think of her as more than a student? Was he watching her the whole time before her exam?

Did he have a lot of pubic hair? What would it feel like to be with someone that isn't Daniel?

In the morning she felt horrible for her lustful thoughts.

By the end of the trip, Macy had relented on trying to help Daniel have fun. Daniel stayed in the room playing on his new handheld gaming device drinking dirty martinis while she went to the pool area. She sat in the Jacuzzi, meeting people from Chechnya and Brazil. She jogged on a treadmill and chatted with a woman from Alaska. She discovered a quiet nook on the bow of the ship to sit and read her latest Wayne Dyer book. She found herself reading the same sentence over and over again. Her head was back in the yoga studio. She hadn't turned a page in her book all afternoon. "Ugh! Stop it!" she said to herself out loud. She went back to their room but Daniel was gone.

They were supposed to go to dinner on the terrace, so Macy got dressed up. When Daniel didn't show up to the room, she wandered around the ship until she spotted him stumbling out of the casino's VIP lounge. He was so drunk that he went back to the room and immediately passed out.

Disembarkation was the next day. Daniel was ready to get off the ship and was irritated at how long the process took. He wanted to skip breakfast and be the first in line to leave.

On the ride home from the dock, Macy called Oona. "Hi Mom. How'd it go with Phoenix?"

Macy's mother filled her in on all the details. After hearing her mother describe Phoenix and their adorable antics, Macy was ready to get home.

She hung up the phone and her thoughts drifted. Suddenly, her phone rang. She didn't recognize the number.

Daniel peered over. "Is that your mom?"

"No. I don't know who it is. I'll let it go to voicemail."

A few moments later her voicemail chimed to let her know there was a new message. She hit the voicemail button and pressed the phone to her ear. A man's soft voice with a thick accent came on the line. "Hi Macy. This is Jakub. I would like to speak with you. Would you call me? Please. 316-1988. Thank you."

Macy couldn't believe he called her. There was a long pause between each of his sentences. He was thinking deeply about every word he spoke. She started shaking. His voice was soft, almost in a whisper. He left his cell phone number. Macy saved the message.

"Who was that?" Daniel asked.

"Wrong number," she answered and closed her eyes for the rest of the ride.

Macy was so happy to see Phoenix when she arrived home. He ran, arms wide open, to welcome her back. She lifted him and twirled him around. As much as she needed the break from him, she needed his little hugs too. He was at the center of her world. His hair was more strawberry than Macy's russet and his skin was pearly.

Macy often felt guilty for not having another child to take the focus off him. She and Daniel were in no place to bring more children into their relationship.

Phoenix let Macy out of his grasp and tackled Daniel at the kitchen door.

"Hey Scooter!" The two wrestled around. Daniel loved Phoenix. Despite being distracted around Macy at times, he was usually present for their child.

After initial hugs, Daniel went straight to grab his tablet. Macy went to bed exhausted that night. The vacation was more work than fun. Sleep escaped her grasp. Macy's head had become a place for her to unleash her fantasies and play them like a movie caught in a loop. As she slowed the scenes and took them moment by moment, she became aroused as if it were all happening again. She got out of bed and retrieved her phone. She listened to Jakub's message eight more times. His accent was unique. He didn't use contractions when he spoke. She was charged with a heightened degree of passion, and her hand met the mouth of her vagina. She never felt her body respond this way to someone's voice. After bringing herself pleasure, she went back to bed and fell into a deep slumber.

Macy did not call Jakub back but she could think of nothing else. He would be out of the country soon; things would be back to normal, she told herself. She elected to put all of that passion and imagination into her marriage. She searched for family-friendly activities around town she and Daniel could take Phoenix to. She poured her creativity into any idea that would bring them closer. She read an article about gluten intolerance leading to headaches and looked up recipes that would eliminate gluten from Phoenix's diet. She wore her hair the way Daniel liked and tried new perfume.

But the harder she tried, the more distant Daniel seemed. Nothing jarred Daniel's financial focus. He continued to analyze the grocery bills and complained when she returned with the week's food. Macy felt guilty for not doing better research on sales and clipping coupons. Daniel's travel steadily increased.

Macy had never been to a mental health professional before. She considered that to be for people with real problems…but she was starting to consider herself as one of those people. She felt like she was losing her mind. She made an appointment with her gynecologist and requested a blood panel to analyze her hormones. After the results indicated she was balanced, she started researching their insurance benefits for a physiotherapist. Maybe she needed to be on medication.

She made an appointment with a therapist named Dr. Smithson. At first, Macy timidly chatted with the counselor. The therapist chipped away at the façade, enabling Macy to get real. The more Macy spoke to the counselor, the angrier she got. Speaking about their relationship spelled it all out. It was like she was taking things out of her pocket and laying it on the table to analyze. Dr. Smithson helped Macy see some of their behaviors were not healthy or normal.

"It seems to me that there may be some deception going on, Macy," the counselor said. "I'm not comfortable saying more than that until I meet with Daniel. Could you bring him in with you?"

Daniel refused to go to counseling with Macy. So, Macy took drastic measures, moving out of their bedroom even though Daniel was rarely home. Phoenix noticed how unhappy everyone was. Their lives were unraveling.

One morning Macy stayed in her bed—not because she was sleeping, but because the pain of facing another day was too much. She refused to get up and take Phoenix to school so Daniel was left with no option but to take over. That day Daniel reluctantly agreed to attend a therapy session with Macy.

During their first session, Macy confronted Daniel about the PayPal account.

Daniel became defensive. "What about my privacy here? This is your fault. She's making a mountain out of a molehill."

Macy had never been so forthcoming before. She was good at harboring her feelings, not expressing them. Now she was angry at how he belittled her abilities to make decisions. She felt undervalued and taken for granted. She realized how unskilled she was at communicating. Neither of them had the tools to negotiate through healthy conversations. Speaking her truth with Dr. Smithson gave Macy a new freedom.

Dr. Smithson encouraged Daniel to give Macy some space by separating.

"Wait a minute, I thought you were supposed to be helping us save our marriage, not driving a wedge further between us. Don't you have some trick? A few thrusts to the sternum to revive this thing? CPR for relationships?"

The counselor explained that space might help him save their marriage. "Daniel, I'm hearing that you are angry right now."

Daniel disagreed with her tactic. Macy was just as surprised. She wondered how she would manage everything without Daniel around.

"I just don't see how separating can help us reconcile our relationship," Daniel said. "What do you want me to do? Move out? Away from my son? It's absurd! Just a few months ago she was hounding me to have another baby and now you want me to move out? What kind of a wack-a-doo did you bring me to, Macy? You broke into my account and you're making assumptions."

Dr. Smithson continued to type on her laptop. The therapist finally spoke. "Daniel, I hear what you're saying. You're angry at my suggestion. Macy's desire for another baby in this marriage was a desperate cry to bring the two of you closer. Your marriage is broken. My suggestion for you two to separate might be the only way you can save your relationship."

He looked like a prisoner of war who had just been subjected to hours of interrogation. His head dropped to his hands. He looked defeated and thinner than she remembered. She worried about his health. His weight had fluctuated for months.

Daniel eventually relented, "Well, I've never been to a therapist before."

There was a long pause.

"But you're the professional, so, whatever. I guess."

A week later, Daniel planned a trip to visit Pat and his friends in California. When he returned, he moved out of the family home and Macy made the painful decision to put Mukha to rest.

20

"And life's like an hourglass, glued to the table
No one can find the rewind button, girl
So cradle your head in your hands
And breathe, just breathe."
– Anna Nalick

Macy got the credit card bill from the week Daniel was in California. He had dined at expensive restaurants, made charges late night, and stayed at a hotel for a night. After a week with Pat in California, Daniel moved into a rental house about twenty minutes away.

Macy hated being alone at night. She had nothing to look forward to in the evenings. Daniel was never much fun when he trekked down the stairs and sat at the head of the table ready to be fed dinner, but she was used to adult company when he wasn't traveling. At first she tried to pretend Daniel was on a business trip. The separation seemed to be going better for Daniel than Macy. He was being more social with friends and started working out again. Macy felt dowdy and unattractive. Adding to her loneliness, Mukha was gone.

Daniel came to pick up Phoenix every other weekend. Occasionally Macy would drop him off there. Phoenix's room at Daniel's was decorated with Scooby Doo and Star Wars posters. Macy never went inside but Phoenix told her about it. Phoenix was resilient.

Daniel's parents were the last to know about the couple's separation. The Westcotts were planning to visit on a weekend Daniel had Phoenix at his new house. Now everyone would know.

One day, Daniel came to pick up Phoenix to spend the weekend with him. The Westcotts were visiting and Phoenix was excited to go out to dinner with them.

"Hey Scooter! Grandma and Grandpa are coming. They're taking you to dinner tomorrow night." Daniel fluffed his hair.

"Yay!" Phoenix danced. "Are you coming too, Dad?"

"I have a business dinner but we're going to order pizza tonight."

"Yes!" Phoenix high-fived his dad.

Daniel left his tablet on the counter where Macy was washing dishes. The boys went upstairs to pack an overnight bag when Daniel's tablet made an audible alert that a text was received. Macy leaned over the bar and considered unlocking the tablet to see what the text was. She knew he had a passcode on it, but she was curious about the combination of numbers he might use to protect his privacy. She wondered if it would be his birthday, the last four digits in his social security number, their address, their anniversary, Phoenix's birthday…. She wondered how many times she could try before getting locked out. She knew she was being nosy, but she couldn't resist.

She looked over her shoulder. Her tongue came to the corner of her mouth as she listened for their voices. She could hear they were in Phoenix's room. She patted her fingers dry on a dishtowel and flipped the tablet's protective case open.

Just as she opened the case, a picture flew out from the inside pocket and landed on the floor. Macy blinked as she leaned down to pick it up. It was a picture of Daniel and Pat surrounded by topless women with a sign that read *Sky Adult Bar*. Daniel had one arm around a tall blonde with huge breasts. His hand reached toward her yellow G-string. Pat was smiling cockeyed with the half-glazed look Macy was familiar with.

Macy stood in the kitchen with the water flowing over the dishes and spilling onto the floor. Once the water splashed her toes, she snapped out of her trance, replaced the picture, and closed the tablet case without even attempting to read the text message. She quickly cleaned up her mess as Daniel and Phoenix came down the stairs.

"Tell Mommy goodbye," Daniel encouraged Phoenix.

"Bye Mommy!"

Daniel grabbed his things and left. Macy stood at the kitchen sink for what felt like hours. Her head throbbed. In one moment her life was so different than the one before. She felt like a zombie on autopilot finishing the dishes. She checked her pulse. For a moment she thought her heart was going to stop beating altogether. While her stomach was in knots, her heartbeat was sustainably unchanged. It was in that moment that she knew her feelings for Daniel had transformed. She wasn't jealous. She wasn't feeling rage. There was a sting but it wasn't a longing to be back with him. It was disgust. Other than that…nothing.

The next morning, Macy made two phone calls. The first was to Dr. Smithson. She explained what had happened. Her counselor encouraged Macy to come in with Daniel and discuss what she had found. Macy flat out refused.

"I feel numb," she told her counselor.

"You are emotionally cutting off, Macy. That's a normal reaction. I would urge you to be honest with Daniel about seeing the picture and schedule an appointment as soon as you can."

Macy argued, "I don't think you understand. He's hiring whores. I'm not jealous—I'm *numb*. I'm done. I'm not coming back to counseling. I'm done with him. I'm done with counseling. I'm done with video games. I want my youth back. I want the days when we saw stars in each other's eyes. I'm done with the controlling and condescending words. *I am done.*"

Dr. Smithson tried to talk sense into Macy. "You might be jumping to conclusions, Macy. I'm afraid you're being rash, dear."

Macy hung up on Dr. Smithson.

The second call Macy made was to Daniel.

"I saw the text between you and Pat," Macy bluffed, "and the picture in your device. Nice picture, by the way. Your girlfriend's tits are just fabulous."

Daniel's reaction was predictable. "Hey, you and Dr. Smithson are the ones who suggested we separate, Macy. Not me. I was fine in our marriage. We're separated. What do you want me to do? I didn't want any of this. Do you think I wanted to pay a mortgage *and* rent? I tried to talk you both out of this insane idea."

"Again with the money?" She laughed bitterly. "We were supposed to be working on our marriage. Not destroying it completely by screwing a woman at a bar or a paid whore."

Daniel's silence was equivalent to an admission. Now Macy *did* feel something. She was pissed. His silence made her angrier. She continued.

"Well, now I don't want any of this, Daniel. I don't want any of it! You can be with your video games and your whores at the Sky Adult Bar. I'm not reconciling with you. It's over. And you can keep all your fucking money. I know you spent hundreds of dollars on your other credit cards and I was stupid to believe that condom was a joke from a tradeshow. You're living a double life."

"You need to calm down, Macy. You're taking things out of context. The text was just guy talk. Nothing major happened. Yes, I have other credit cards and yes, I go to titty bars; yes, I've used an escort service but I can explain. I think we should talk."

Macy slammed her phone down so hard it cracked the screen.

A second later, the phone rang. Macy knew Daniel would call back, but through the shattered screen, she recognized a different number. It was her brother.

"Ugh. Not now."

Macy had not spoken to her brother in months. How could she tell him about something so intimate and embarrassing? She was in no frame of mind to catch up with him now. She let the call go to her voicemail.

Her phone rang again. It was her brother.

What in the world? Macy thought. She exhaled a sigh and sat back, letting her voicemail pick up once more.

21

"There she was like a picture.
There she was, she was just the same.
There she was."
– Adonis

As she watched her brother's name come up on her caller ID for the third time, Macy had a strange feeling in the pit of her stomach.

"Hello?" she stammered.

Her brother sounded exhausted. "Macy. It's Dad." His voice cracked. "He was working on a car in the heat and went into cardiac arrest and dropped."

"What?! Is he okay now? Is he at the hospital? Where is he?" she pressed in disbelief.

"Macy…."

There was a long pause.

"…Dad is dead."

The ground shifted beneath Macy's feet. Her knees gave out. She caught herself on the island. She could not comprehend the sentences that followed—the words were garbled up meaningless phrases. Like rotten teeth, the words fell out of his mouth each time he spoke, but Macy could not understand them.

Macy slowly walked up her stairs. She gingerly leaned on the banister for help as she pulled her weight each step leading to the master bedroom. She numbly sat on the bed. Macy's beloved father had died.

The shift that occurred in Macy was monumental. Her mind quickly played scenes from her childhood like a movie, all the things he had done. Throwing her in the pool so high she could see the top of the high diving board. Holding the back of the banana seat, running along beside her when she learned to ride without training wheels. Showing up at her school when she needed stitches from a fall off the monkey bars. Catching her wearing blush after going through Oona's makeup kit. Scaring the stray dog away that attacked her at the bus stop early one morning. To this day, he didn't know she had seen the roaming dog before she left for school and put salami in her pocket to feed the animal. Carl always seemed to show up out of the shadows when she most needed him. Who would do that for her now? Not Daniel.

In a matter of hours, she had lost the two most important men in her life. She thought of the first time she saw her Dad cry—when he walked her down the aisle. When Phoenix was born, his presence gave her the most comfort. Macy realized time was fleeting and she was getting old.

Macy sat on the edge of her bed thinking of how she would die. It seemed preposterous to think it wouldn't happen. Yet in all the years she had prepared for her parents' death, she somehow believed they were immortal. She saw photographs on the wall of a couple young, in love and smiling. She didn't know who those people were. She felt empty.

For the first time in years, she felt uncertain of who she was or how to define herself.

She crawled into a fetal position. Ordinarily, Mukha would jump up to comfort her. Now, he was dead too. As she sobbed, Macy thought of how hollow Oona must be feeling without Carl.

Mom needs some time before she can talk. She will call you in a while, a text message from her brother said.

She lay in a ball and thought of death. She held her breath to see how it would feel not to breathe. She thought of her father decomposing in the ground and her body surged with emotions. She hiccupped and sobbed for an hour. Macy prayed for the inspiration to go on another day. She thought of Phoenix. She wanted to talk to him, to tell him how much she loved him, but she was too unstable. Macy didn't know who to call or who to reach out to for comfort.

She scanned her memories for a lifeline. Someone who could help this go away.

A rush of adrenaline took her limbs hostage. Her heart rate increased. She picked her phone up and looked through the cracked screen. She went to her voicemail log. Almost a year had passed since she got that call from Jakub. She began to pant looking for his message. Her hands shook as they wrote down his phone number. She would write Jakub's number down, she decided, and think about contacting him. Looking down through her crushed cell phone screen, she surprised herself when she pressed *Return Call*.

"Hello?" His voice was soft, yearning for an answer, expectant. He answered on the first ring. "Macy?" he whispered lightly.

She could tell by the ache in his tone that he was emotional. In one word, she could tell he had a million questions and answers waiting for her in this conversation. Macy's eyes were a blur and she said nothing.

"Are you okay?" he said with his thick accent.

His voice cascaded through her ears and smoothed over her shoulders. She could tell by the inflection in his voice he wanted to know how she was feeling, if she was upset, if she had thought about him every moment as he had thought about her. He wanted to know as much as she could tell him. Part of her wished they didn't have things like caller ID so she could hang up and call back just to hear him say hello again.

"Macy? I know it's you. I can feel it." His voice dropped off as he pressed the phone closely to his ear, waiting to receive her response.

"You know it's me because you have caller ID."

A gust of air came from his mouth as he chuckled. "I know it is you because I have felt you in my soul since the first day I touched you," he said matter-of-factly.

"I have thought about you…about what happened," she said. She calmed herself and spoke softly.

He exhaled for several seconds. "I think of you every hour of every day, Macy. How do you feel when you think about what happened?"

Intrigued by his blunt question, she answered just as directly, "Reckless, confused, excited. I congratulate myself on the days I don't think about the night of my final exam."

It felt good to admit that. She didn't realize it until she said it out loud, but it was true. She had thought of Jakub daily since he kissed her. She celebrated the days that passed when she didn't have a fragmented memory pierce through her brain.

They were quiet. It was if he was waiting for her to share the news.

"Jakub, my father died today." Speaking the words made it real.

The phone was quiet.

When Jakub finally started speaking, his words were so fast Macy had trouble understanding him. He slipped into his native tongue.

"What?" she asked several times. "Can you repeat that please?"

His tone was urgent but Macy couldn't understand his English through his accent over the phone. She didn't realize how much easier it was to understand him when she could see his eyes.

He spoke slowly, "I will pack my things now. I will take the first available flight from Toronto. I can be in the United States tomorrow. Meet me tomorrow…please." He said it with such burning intensity that she finally understood.

"What!? Tomorrow? Where?" She was surprised that he would drop everything to be with her, especially after so many months had passed. She was flattered and excited that he would make her a priority this way.

"I will text the address and time of my arrival. I will be there for you soon, Macy. I am sorry about your father. He must have been a remarkable man to have raised you."

Macy's heart was pounding through her chest like a captive bird.

Jakub threw her a lifeline.

22

"They say I'll be OK
But I'm not going to ever get over you."
– Miranda Lambert

Macy's mind went back to her father. She wondered how Oona was coping. She lay back on her bed feeling exhausted. She was glad Daniel had Phoenix this weekend. She didn't know how she was going to tell him about his grandfather.

Her phone rang. *Mom at Home* came on the display. She took a breath knowing she was about to have the hardest conversation of her life.

Macy's eyes filled like a water trough. Hearing her mother's voice allowed the tears to release. Oona was a strong woman but she just lost her best friend. She was a wreck. Macy wanted to make everything okay. She wanted everything to be the way it had been just days before. She wanted to revert to childhood. She wanted her daddy.

Macy packed a bag and went to Oona's house. She answered calls, organized food, made arrangements. The doorbell rang constantly. Sleeping at her parents' house without her father there felt eerie. She morbidly wondered where Carl's soul was and if he was near. Her worst nightmare as a child had finally come to fruition. Her father wasn't going to take another breath and make everything alright.

She climbed into her orange sweatpants and cried into her pillow. She asked her spirit guides to help guide Carl during his transition into the non-physical realm.

Just before she closed her eyes, Macy felt the presence of her father. She spoke out loud, "I love you, Daddy. I miss you so much. I wish you were still here. I know you're fixing cars with grease on your fingers, playing the guitar, and singing."

She was comforted with images of her father that warmed her heart. She slept.

That night Macy had a confusing emotional dream. It was Halloween. She was trick-or-treating on the same street she grew up on back in California. But now she was an adult. She had a big costume on that made her unrecognizable. She was a man-sized butterfly. She was holding hands with a little boy. This was the same boy from her dream after her night with Jakub. He looked like Phoenix, but he was different.

"Nicholas, let's get candy from this house." She felt an urgency to take her child trick-or-treating at that particular house. The streets were crowded with children in costume and most parents were dressed up too.

"Nicholas, ring the doorbell and say trick-or-treat."

He obliged her request. Nicholas rang the bell. The door opened. Jakub was on the other side of the threshold. Macy gasped inside her costume to see his face. He was older. Nicholas blinked at the man and remembered his lines.

"Twick-or-Tweet."

Jakub bent down and looked closely at the boy and tilted his head. "Hello. You look familiar. Do I know you?"

Macy woke up sobbing before the sun came up.

The next morning when Oona joined her in the kitchen, Macy had already made scrambled eggs, toast, and tea. They watched the sunrise from the front porch. They spoke in quiet voices. They discussed what kind of funeral service they would arrange. Carl's will gave specific instructions to cremate his body and spread his ashes in the ocean. The service would be the following day. Macy couldn't believe her mother was talking about arrangements for her father's funeral.

The day was a stream of phone calls from preachers, neighbors, former mechanics, and old hunting buddies. When an address was texted to Macy's phone, she was slightly confused. She scrolled down and saw the message with it. It simply said:

I understand if you can't make it or wish not to see me at this time but I am here for you as long as you want.

Macy knew the message was from Jakub and was written with care. Her brothers were there and the house was full. Macy knew it would be hardest for Oona when the visitors were gone and daily life resumed. She calculated the distance between Oona's home and the address Jakub texted her.

The map indicated she wasn't far from the address. It was between her parents' house and Macy's town. She was relieved she could get away easily but felt a pang of guilt at how crazy this was. She couldn't believe she was actually going to see Jakub again.

Macy told Oona she was going home to shower and pack a few things. Oona was so occupied that she waved Macy off. "Of course, darling. Take your time coming back tomorrow. The service isn't until 2:00 PM. Maybe we can caravan to the beach."

"Tomorrow?!" Macy exclaimed. "Don't you want me to come and spend the night again tonight, Mom?"

"Well, I thought your brothers could stay in the guest room, honey. Is that okay?"

"Oh, yes of course. You'll be okay?"

"Your dad wouldn't leave a feeble old woman who can't take care of herself. He knew I'd be okay." Oona put on a brave front.

Macy sat in her car for a few moments looking into her parents' house. A sentimental ache grew in her heart. Lights shined from the inside. She could see her brothers milling around the living room. The trees and shrubs were larger...older like her. Grief rose in her belly. Memories flooded her mind. Desperate to distract her sadness, she looked down at the map on her phone and studied the route to Jakub.

So much had changed in twenty-four hours. One day ago she still had her father and a chance at saving her marriage. How could so much impact her world so quickly? How would she feel when she saw Jakub? How would he feel? Did he really *feel* her and think about her? Maybe she would see him and feel nothing. She was confused and wanted clarity. Things never felt resolved from their last encounter.

It would be good to finally talk about what happened.

23

"I wanna rock your gypsy soul
just like way back in the days of old
then magnificently we will float
into the mystic."
– Van Morrison

Macy drove following directions just outside of town. Landscape lights led the way to a street lined with magnolia trees. The large Southern bed and breakfast boasted a wraparound porch outfitted with rocking chairs and a swing. Through the limbs of the largest magnolia tree she had ever seen, Macy instantly recognized this place. It was where she had been in the accident.

She saw a figure sitting on the porch swing. "Oh my God. It's him." Macy's heart rate soared.

She turned into the entrance. The front tires hit the long gravel driveway and everything went into slow motion. She glanced at herself in the rearview mirror and looked back to the swing.

Jakub recognized her car and stood up from the swing. He wore a long-sleeved light blue button-up shirt and khaki pants. She parked and stood outside her car, gently closed the door, paused, and looked up to see him twenty feet away. Their eyes locked as they slowly ambled toward each other.

Macy's legs felt like they were trudging through water. There was no time, no space, no gravity to make sense of things. The air surrounding them was charged when she stopped two feet from him. They examined each other's expression, searching one another's eyes.

In one gesture, Jakub flipped his palm open and lifted it toward her. Macy drew in a sharp breath as she escaped from her frozen hold and burst forward into his open arms. He caught her in his strong embrace and cradled her head and back. One lonely tear rolled down his face.

Macy grazed ecstasy in his arms. He broke their embrace only to hold the back of her neck with his palm, his finger behind her ear and his thumb at her jawline, lifting her head gently.

"Macy. You've come to me. From the moment I saw you, I knew who you were."

Macy didn't understand exactly, but there was no need for words. Her heart fluttered against her chest. She closed her weeping eyes and begged for his kiss. Gently tilting her head toward his, Jakub pressed his lips to hers, sending a chain reaction through every cell of her body. Their mutual tingles felt like angels clapping. When their mouths disconnected, he delicately took her hand and led her up the stairs into the building.

The foyer was large with vaulted ceilings. Immediately to the left was a small coffee shop with a stone fireplace crackling on the far wall. Jakub led Macy to the loveseat that faced the warmth of the fire. He was the only resident of the inn, he said, so privacy was theirs. Their bodies angled toward each other, and neither spoke for a few moments. They watched the shadows of the fire dance across one another's face for a while.

The innkeeper was the first to break the silence. His footsteps grew closer and he peeked in, offering them wine and cheese.

Macy and Jakub spent hours chatting in front of the fire. They shared their thoughts about the night of her final exam when Jakub first kissed Macy. Jakub admitted to observing Macy from the back hall of the yoga boutique in the weeks before their stolen kiss. He had been in deep meditation when a beautiful voice broke his concentration. She hummed as she walked the perimeter of the studio. He was captivated while he watched and listened to her melody.

They talked about how much time they had each spent thinking about the other. Jakub reached for Macy's hand when she shed tears over her father's passing. His tenor was empathetic. He countered her naked honesty by divulging his traumatic past. She was the first person he told about his younger brother Niko and how he died tragically.

The Krakow government banned residents from heating their homes in the evening so Jakub and his siblings slept in the same bed to share body heat. The children would huddle together and shiver through the night. There was no means of birth control. Jakub had eight siblings…and then only seven. Jakub's mother earned a wage by nursing other women's babies. Because his father worked in a bakery, the family had access to a regular food source. Thus, his mother's mammary glands continued to supply milk.

Jakub was especially fond of his youngest brother, Niko, who adored Jakub. He would watch Jakub misbehave and never tattle on him. Niko wanted to be just like Jakub when he got older. As the last and youngest child, Niko went to a public childcare center so his parents could earn wages. These centers were overcrowded with children and rampant with illnesses. There were over one hundred children to only two or three caregivers. Jakub's mother didn't like leaving Niko at the center but the wage for breast milk helped them sustain their livelihood.

One afternoon a messenger was sent to Jakub's home to inform them of horrible news. Little Niko had discovered the custodian's mop and bucket containing bleach. Thirsty and innocent, Niko drank the bleach. By the time his parents and Jakub arrived, the liquid had burned his intestines. His bowels were involuntarily contracting, pushing pieces of his intestines out of his rectum. The sight was gruesome. The pain he experienced was unbearable. Doctors tried to save him, but the bleach was absorbed through the gastrointestinal wall, causing his organs to slowly melt away. Niko lived three more grisly days before renouncing life. Jakub was devastated and his mother never smiled with her eyes again.

That sadness Macy sensed in Jakub was understood now. He admitted that he had always wanted a son so he could name him after his little brother, Niko. They discussed everything from child rearing and potty training to philosophy and religion. He wanted to know everything about Phoenix. He loved how Macy's eyes gleamed when she spoke of her son. He noticed it the first week in his yoga class. Jakub's opinion was that Americans offered the word "love" too frequently. "By America's frequent use of the word, it diminishes the meaning." But he liked how Macy professed her love for Phoenix.

Jakub had never been married. He believed in past life incarnation, karma, soulmates, and twin flames, and stubbornly held to the idea that he had a twin flame during this lifetime. As the night moved on, it was clear they were not going anywhere.

The innkeeper stopped by again to check on them before locking up. He restocked the firewood, opened a second bottle of wine, and left Macy and Jakub in the shadows of their conversation. They sipped from the same glass, fed each other cheese, and told more stories of their past, desires for their future. They were vulnerable, comfortable, honest. Macy's perception of Jakub had been largely based on her experience with him through the yoga course. In the last three hours it evolved. Macy enjoyed hearing about his other passions. He enjoyed carpentry. With a curious eye of a craftsman, he examined things like mosaics, dovetail woodworking, even door hinges. The way materials could be woven together fascinated him. He appreciated raw natural material like tumbled travertine. He repaired antique cars. When he was a child, he dreamed of being a racecar driver.

Macy hung on every one of his words. She imagined giving him a gift of NASCAR racing one day. He was so strong yet so vulnerable.

Macy draped her legs over his lap as the hours pressed on. They never spoke of Daniel. Their fever to be together grew with the heat of the fire. A desire thickened by their heartbeats, by every breath they exhaled, and by the black of the night.

24

"She tied you to her kitchen chair
And she broke your throne and she cut your hair
And from your lips she drew the hallelujah."
— Leonard Cohen

Jakub placed the last grape in Macy's mouth. She couldn't believe how sensual this action was. She was surprised that she didn't feel foolish with a man feeding her grapes. When they finished the second bottle of wine, they sat quietly staring into each other's eyes. They had divulged an unbelievable amount of information to one another.

She felt her body rise to the call of his unspoken request. Jakub became firm and hungry for Macy. He leaked pellets of arousal as he waited for her to agree to his silent appeal. It started as a longing in his center and grew to a yearning. Macy looked into his eyes and imagined the pleasure of receiving him inside her. Her lips plumped up fuller, hungry. His penis grew thick in his pants. Her vagina pulsated as blood surged through her vessels. Her breath caught in her throat. They shared a long passionate kiss with their lips parted just enough to feel the tips of each other's tongue.

She asked one question: "What room are we in?"

He smiled and picked her up, sweeping her in his arms, carried her up two flights of stairs, never breaking eye contact, and nudged the door open with his knee. He tenderly laid Macy down on the bed. She kept her eyes on him as he lit candles all over the room.

He returned to her, hovered over her as if tattooing his brain with the image of her. He delicately and slowly began to unbutton her shirt. Macy's nipples were at attention, her breasts were full and spilling out of her bra. He straddled her body, opened her shirt, and gazed down at her.

"Kocham Cię. Kocham Cię. Kocham Cię. Jestem w tobie zakochany."

Macy didn't understand him, but she loved hearing him speak his native tongue. She also loved hearing him speak English. His pronunciation was easier to decipher now. Hearing him speak Polish gave her a surge of desire.

She placed her hand on his blue shirt and ripped it open. They laughed at the sound of buttons flying off and hitting the hard wood floors.

"Perfection," he murmured.

She rolled him over with a hasty strength of reverence for him. She couldn't wait for him to fill her up. She yearned to envelop him. He returned her enthusiasm, quickly removing her panties.

Suddenly Macy remembered she was on her period. "Oh no!" She motioned to stop him, but he froze her with his look. He was still scrutinizing her with the look of adoration. No one ever looked at her in awe this way before. It was sacred.

In one skilled movement, Jakub pulled Macy's hips to the edge of the bed where her feet dangled to the floor. He slowly kneeled down on the floor so that his eyes were at the same level as her hips. She laid back flat on the bed, her breasts spilling off to her sides. He pressed his finger to her hip and leisurely traced it down to the top of her pubic bone. She was completely exposed. He put light pressure on the inside of her thighs, opening her legs, and saw the string to her tampon. It was the cord to the object that was obstructing his full joy. Like a soldier taking command of his fleet, he began to deliver a coaxing invitation for the tampon to cross the border.

Jakub wiggled the string back and forth from left to right and pulled softly. Macy's vagina was tightly locked around the tampon. He made tiny swirling motions, whirling the string in a circle, almost bringing her to orgasm. Slowly her vagina released its grip, allowing the tampon to exit. She lifted her head in disbelief and searched his eyes for a reaction. He carefully wrapped the tampon as if preparing it for a funeral and stood to discard it in the wastebasket. His penis was so large, just the shiny tip of it busted out of the waistband of his underwear. Expertly, she freed it from captivity and engulfed him in her mouth.

Jakub watched Macy with his penis between her lips. Macy's eyes were closed as she flicked her tongue long against his shaft and swirled off at his tip. When she opened her eyes, they gazed at each other as she continued. In control now, Macy placed his penis between her breasts and encased him, moving with gentle friction up and down.

Jakub couldn't take any more. With a desire paramount to anything he had ever known before, he plunged into her tight vagina, but was only able to fit his tip inside. Macy gasped at his girth. The vastness of his penis was a shock to her frame.

He paused, searching her face. She thought for a moment he might split her straight down the middle. They were frozen and throbbing.

"Breathe," he whispered.

With a long exhale, she released tension from her body. The tight grasp her vagina began to relax, allowing his cock to fully submerge into her. Their hips landed in the same place, their gaze never broke, and they grasped hands. They began to move in perfect harmony. It was ceremonial. It went beyond the tactile physical experience of sex—it was spiritual. It took over their visceral instincts.

Jakub took residence inside of Macy, moving patiently and slowly with full, long strokes the length of his penis. He wanted to remember every detail of her frame, the room, the smells, the lighting. He tilted his head as he moved to the tempo of her heart and memorized her face. She opened her eyes and smiled, allowing him to break her open. At the mercy of the spell he had cast upon her, she had completely relinquished control. Their union contained enough energy to light the entire galaxy.

His long, slow strokes grew into shorter, faster thrusts. She paused to trace his eyebrow with her thumb and commit the moment to memory. Then she dug her fingernails into the back of his hand. A yearning developed to make it last forever. They took each other to the edge of euphoria and stopped just before arriving only to rapture each other in bliss again. There was an overwhelming sense of oneness that occurred when she held him inside. Pressing themselves into each other's delight felt like coming home.

This was a passion that charged Macy's insides—something she had never considered possible. Jakub's goal was not about having an orgasm; it was his admiration of the landscape. He relished every moment of being inside her. He savored every word of her drunken stream of consciousness. He moved to it like a dance.

"How do you innately know how to touch me like this?" she gasped.

"Your body tells me."

It was the perfect reply. He answered the call of her mind and body and delivered her pleasure in unspeakable ways. Jakub wanted all of Macy. He lifted his chest off hers, pressed his hand against her sternum, and closed his eyes to listen to their hearts' connection. He continued to gently thrust his hips. He held his hand to her ribs.

"It is the perfect triangle."

He placed his fingers intermittently between each of her ribs and memorized her frame as if he may never feel her skin again. She placed her hand on top of his and felt with him.

"You are the one I have been waiting for. You are not just my ultimate soulmate; you are my twin flame. This is why I never wanted to marry anyone before you. I have been waiting for you for lifetimes," he murmured. She studied him and captured the image of his face in her mind. "I would wait a million more lifetimes just to hold you for a moment in time."

After hours of flooding mutual pleasure on each other, Macy and Jakub rose to a climax neither could deny. With fingers threaded, they erupted in simultaneous orgasms. The way her vagina contracted after her orgasm reminded him of an erratic heartbeat, speaking its own version of Morse code. Their hands tightened around each other.

He waited for her body to stop convulsing. "I love you, Em."

"Em." Short for the M in Macy—and she understood it immediately. He was the only one who had ever called her "Em." It came so naturally. All four of those words put together were magic.

"What did you say?" she asked just to be clear she wasn't dreaming.

He looked into her soul. "I love you, Em."

She smiled with the deepest gratitude in her heart. She shifted her body so that she was sitting up on him, his penis still inside her, her legs straddled on each side of his hips.

"I love you, Jakub."

Feeling overwhelmed with things she'd never felt, she lunged forward with urgency to press her mouth against his. Her long hair swept across his face. A single strand fell in his mouth as they exchanged souls with a kiss. She leaned back and looked at him. His mouth was moving and he swallowed.

"What were you doing?" she asked curiously with a tilt of her head.

"Your hair fell in my mouth. I swallowed it so I can have your DNA inside of me."

Candlelight danced across their faces. Their eyes still connected. His penis grew softer but remained long inside her. The level of intimacy between them had crossed a new threshold. They collapsed into each other's naked vulnerability.

Jakub held her with conviction through the night. He never let her out of his loving embrace. Any time she moved, he quietly moaned and pulled her closer as if she escaped, she would never come back.

Off and on the two woke up in each other's exposed vulnerability. They fell in and out of a delicious semi-conscious sleep, where dreams and consciousness are inseparable realities. They basked in their nakedness. They came to awareness, snuggled tighter, moaned, looked deeply into each other's eyes, and fell back asleep. When they slipped into dream state, their tangled up arms would loosen just slightly. He would rouse and snuggle her more closely, burrow his nose deeply into the nape of her neck. She would wake gently and wiggle her backside to him, pressing more firmly into his penis. He lifted her hair and kissed just under her neckline. Macy had a fleeting thought that if she died now, she would die happy. Really happy. Just to bask in his arms this way—nothing could compare to the serenity she felt on this night.

It was still dark outside but the sun considered its emergence. Macy turned over to face him now. The lovers stared each other in the eyes. Jakub pressed his hand to Macy's sternum and closed his eyes.

"I'm trying to memorize your heart's song so I can sing it to you when we meet in our next lifetime. I don't want to wait this long for you to recognize me again." His other hand found her rib cage and cupped the ribs under her breast. "It's a perfect triangle. You make me weird, you know that? I'm so weird. Why did I say such a weird thing?"

Macy giggled at his humor. She loved the way his eyes slanted up when he smiled.

She felt the match strike her inspiration again. Moments later she wiggled down beneath the sheet where her lips enclosed the tip of his penis. She made tiny circles with her tongue from the tip to its base. Her movements were exquisitely choreographed to the sound of his breath. As his inhales became more turbulent, her mouth became wilder. She dove in deeper and further, licking and sucking the fullness of him to the back of her mouth. His breathing quickened. Macy slurped with starving abandon. Only he could quench her thirst. She wanted all of him in her mouth. She drew his testicles in with her tongue. She drove him close to the cliff of elation and slowed, then again and again. She eased him up the crescendo and down the decrescendo in her musical score. Her technique was the perfect answer to his needs. He was the music; she was the lyrics. Together they were rhythm. He was present in every cell in his body—loving her with every pore of his skin.

He needed her badly. He wanted her to wash him with her blood. He wanted her vagina all over him. They took turns rambling sacred words: "I love you." "I want to devour you." "I want this to last forever." "I want you longer." "I want you forever." "I never want this to end."

Macy was overwhelmed by the familiar scent of home. When she broke free to look in his eyes, she thought forever wouldn't be enough time to love him. She was returning home. "I never want to stop feeling you inside of me. I love you. Oh my God, I love you, Jakub. Wait, not yet. I want to savor you."

He smiled and gladly obliged her with a break and pulled himself out of her. Jakub referred to Macy's vagina as if it was its own entity.

"She's so beautiful," he said. "I love how her folds are held so tightly together. I want to marry you, Macy."

She responded, "Take me away. Bring me to your countryside and teach me your language. Let me watch you create with your hands. Let me write a song to the cadence of your heart." His heart leapt when she spoke of a future with him.

Macy was dressed in nothing but her scars and he adored her vulnerability. When he could no longer take the pain of not being inside her, he held her hands with a firm authority and dove back inside of her glory. She clawed him closer, shoved him deeper, engulfed him completely—and even then she wanted more. She loved hearing him speak. He spoke in analogies to convey his meaning.

"You are tough like a lion on the outside but you are a butterfly in here." He placed his hand on her ribs. "I love you, Em. I love your genes. I want *our* genes. I want to dance so that my sunflower latches to your genes. I want you to have my baby."

The sentiment stunned her. For a moment she wanted to grow his DNA inside her. It was the craziest thing she had ever heard. She could think of no other way to be closer to him than to feel his heartbeat inside her belly.

They whispered on and on for hours making love. He brought her to orgasm with the power of his words alone. And then again with his hand. And then again with his mouth until she had no strength left. When she thought she could handle no more, he would move out of her and hold her hand. Nothing else touching except the sensitive interior of their fingers weaved together like a mosaic. In that singular touch he could drive her to cum again. Then he would enter her and allow himself to go limp there in the warmth of her constricting vagina.

They fell asleep tangled up in each other's web of passion, legs intertwined. Macy's hair flowed over his shoulder. The waves danced freely, falling like a waterfall over his neck. She counted his breaths on her cheek until she gave into exhaustion and slept.

25

*"If I lay here
If I just lay here
Would you lie with me and just forget the world?"
— Snow Patrol*

Macy had wild dreams about her and Jakub dancing in her kitchen. Suddenly a little boy burst in the room. The boy was younger than Phoenix, but looked like him. "Tattie! Tattie!" he called for Jakub.

Macy jumped, waking herself from sleep. Jakub pulled her closer and comforted her with the escape of his light moan.

There was a light knock at the door. The innkeeper left a breakfast tray by the door and padded away. Jakub's hair was pressed into his scalp. At first he had an innocent disorientation on his face. His eyes focused on Macy and happiness quickly sprang to his eyes. He got out of bed to retrieve their breakfast. He was very comfortable being naked in front of her. Macy sneaked a look at his penis as he walked confidently over to open the door. Even at rest, his penis was thick and long. She quickly covered up her exposed breasts. He prepared her tea with agave.

As he went to hand her the cup, he froze. The way the sunlight hit the blue of her eyes astonished him.

"They are like marbles. Your eyes. They are like glass-blown sea-colored marbles. Stunning." He handed her the hot tea. "Good morning."

She accepted the tea and sipped it gingerly. "How did you know how I like my tea?"

"I pay attention to details," he responded with a sly smile.

"Oh really?" she tested.

"Oh really," he quipped in response.

"Then, what was I wearing the first day we met? What's my favorite hobby? And how do I like my steak prepared?"

He smiled from his eyes, eager to play her game. "You had a blue bandana around your head. Your shirt was a white sleeveless snug tank; your yoga pants were blue and white stripes. It would appear by a layman's eye that you did not have nail polish on, but in fact it was a very pale pink. As for hobbies, your voice is that of an angel, and your fingers pluck guitar strings. Because of your level of capability, I would not call it a hobby. You could be a famous music artist. And for your steak…you like it rare. Because you rarely eat meat. Only to be polite in social situations. You would never order it at a restaurant and you never purchase it to cook. Let's see…what else…ah, you menstruate the second week of every month." He took a sip of her tea and raised his eyebrow to her and smirked. Macy's jaw had become unhinged.

Macy sat up, trying to keep herself covered. Jakub grabbed his button-down and wrapped it around her, giving her privacy. "Thank you."

"Well, it is no good to me now. You may keep it. All of the buttons have gone missing. I do not know what happened."

They laughed. Macy was famished and ate all the French toast prepared by the innkeeper. The note on the tray read, *Enjoy your stay. The entire west wing will be vacant through the week. Enjoy a late check out.*

The reality of the day was setting in. Jakub instantly knew where her mind had gone. She had spoken of her father with great sadness the night before. He knew she wished she could crawl under the covers and pretend she was a child.

They stood beside each other, brushing their teeth as if they had been doing it for years. She watched him in the reflection of the bathroom mirror. He was thorough. Each tooth received equal attention from the bristle. When he was done, instead of spitting, he rinsed his toothbrush off with water and stuck it back inside his mouth and scooped out the bubbles on his brush. He rinsed the bristle and brushed more. He repeated this technique until there were no suds in his mouth. He realized Macy was watching so he made a big gesture pushing his eyebrows up and sucked loudly on the brush, contracting his cheeks like a fish. Macy laughed easily. She pushed her stomach out as far as she could, turned to the side so he could see her protruding tummy, and pulled it back in quickly. They laughed at each other's antics.

"I am so weird," he said.

"I make you weird."

"You make me weird," he said with his thick accent. "I like being weird with you."

Macy shyly hung up the blue shirt with missing buttons outside of the shower and stepped in. She took several deep breaths, inhaling the warm mist. The steam quickly created condensation down the glass surrounding. Her mind was swinging like a pendulum. She couldn't believe she had just shared a night of magic with Jakub. They had exchanged so much information in such a short time. They had just studied each other's imperfections in the bathroom mirror and felt completely comfortable. They even used the word "love" for their feelings.

The shower door opened. Macy instinctively sucked her stomach in and covered her breasts.

Jakub gazed at Macy, inhaling her beauty. She instantly relaxed her hands and abdominals. *How did he do that?* she wondered. The way he looked at her felt like he was pouring love over her body like the water from the shower.

"May I come in?" he asked. Without waiting for a response, he stepped into the shower and put soap on a sponge. He took Macy's hips and turned her 180 degrees away from him. He gently took each of her hands and placed them high up against the glass. He lifted her hair and twisted it in a bun on top of her head. When it was secure, he began making little circles with the loofa on the back of her neck. He moved down her shoulders, back, butt, hamstrings, and calves. He lifted each foot, one at a time, covering each sole with suds, and worked his way back up the front side of Macy's naked body.

"This is how we prepare a warrior for battle. The last day they may see one another, they bathe every inch of each other."

Macy felt the swirling of butterflies in her belly. She felt his admiration for her as clearly as she felt the water trickle down her skin. He rinsed her and held a towel for her, wrapping her gently. He swaddled another one around her hair. Then he gently dried her body until she was barely damp, then he held up his blue shirt for her. He tied it in a knot just above her navel and left her to her privacy. She never felt more treasured.

By 10:00 AM, Macy was dressed and ready to leave but she felt a strong sense of nostalgia. She didn't want to leave Jakub. She didn't want to leave the room or the inn. She wanted to hide away there forever. Macy and her family would drive over two hours away to spread Carl's ashes in the tide.

Jakub didn't want to let her go. As if she would never come back, he asked if he could follow her all the way to the beach.

"I want to know you arrive there safely. I want to know everything about you."

Reluctant but excited, she agreed. He stayed back several cars behind hers. He memorized her license plate, where there was a dent, how the tires were balding. He wanted to know every part of her.

When she arrived safely parked at the beach, he did a U-turn and drove back to the inn, respecting her time with her family.

Spreading her father's ashes was the second saddest event of Macy's life. The first was seeing Oona deal with his loss. She was a widow now. Macy ached for her mother more than she did for herself. Oona and Carl shared an incredible relationship and decades of life together. They had more time as a couple than as individuals, and Macy didn't know how Oona would define her world now. After the funeral, Macy was exhausted. She texted Jakub.

> I think I just need some time with my family. I hope you understand.

His response came through immediately.

> Of course. You are a sunflower. When your sun shines again, you will tilt your head to me and allow me to shower you with rays of my love.

Macy turned off her phone and gave her full attention to her grieving mother and brothers. She took care of everything. She organized the food that was in constant flow to Oona's house. She coordinated visits, wrote thank you notes, washed clothes and sheets. Flowers poured in. One large bouquet was from Daniel. The card read, *Oona and Macy, please know I am thinking of you. I am so sorry to hear about Carl. He was like a father to me. Please let me know if I can do anything to ease your pain. All of my love always, Daniel.*

Oona told Macy she was welcome to go home, but Macy refused to leave her mother. Her brothers were gone now and she didn't want her mother to be alone.

"Honey, I'm going to have to be alone sometime. It might as well be now."

Macy shot back, "Well, maybe *I* don't want to be alone, Mom."

Oona knew Macy and Daniel had separated, but she was holding onto hope the two would reconcile. "Well, you could call Daniel," she suggested. "You know he's called me several times to check on me. He's hoping you're doing okay too. He was kind enough to offer to keep Phoenix this week for you. Isn't that nice? He even took Phoenix to the neurologist to see about those headaches."

Macy was aware. Daniel had texted her a couple of sentences. *I'm sorry to hear about Carl,* his message had said. *Anything I can do? How do you wanna tell Phoenix? I'll keep him with me if you need more time.* It didn't appear to be a heartfelt message—at least not with the tone Macy read it.

"No, Mom. You've had a rough day and I don't want to add to it, but to be clear, Daniel and I are *not* getting back together."

Oona looked sadder than she did at the beach. "You know Macy, I just lost the best man I have ever known. I can't tell you how much I took him for granted. The way he set my coffee mug out at night with a spoon and a package of sweetener beside it. He did that even though he doesn't drink coffee. It's a small example of the things he did to enrich my life. He took such good care of me. He left cash in my pocketbook because I never carried any. Just today I discovered he had taken my car and filled it with a full tank of gas. Oh gosh, just the way he looked after you kids. His adoration of Phoenix…. He loved that child as much as he loved you. He was so concerned about Phoenix and his headaches…." She laughed. "If you only knew how he worried about each of you. You were always in the forefront of his mind. Saving money for your wedding or college education. He had the most integrity of any man I have ever known. But he wasn't always that way. He had his moments. What I learned early in our marriage is that you can't tie your happiness to someone else. It's not fair to either person. No one can make you unhappy unless you give them permission to. You must tether your happiness to the sun because whether you can see it or not, it's always there. Some days you will have to travel through turbulent clouds to get to the other side, but when you do, it's even sweeter to experience."

Then, she replaced that sadness with a glimmer of hope in her eye. They were both silent before Oona spoke again. "Sometimes two people have to fall apart to realize how much they need to fall back together."

26

"Only love, only love can hurt like this
Only love can hurt like this
Must have been a deadly kiss
Only love can hurt like this."
— Pamlona Faith

The next morning, over the course of many texts, Jakub expressed his desire to meet Phoenix. Macy texted him:

> Not yet. He's been through so much. We need more time. I haven't even told him about his grandfather yet. Please be patient.

When Macy finally returned home, Daniel pulled into the driveway right after her. Phoenix got out of the car.

"Mommy!" Phoenix ran to Macy. His book bag bounced on his back. "Mommy, I got to go to school from Daddy's. We had donuts for breakfast. It was awesome! We had a pillow fight until I got a headache and lost my balance. Then I went to school and got out early! Daddy took me to a doctor who put wires on my head and we made faces in the mirror. They had cool toys too. Then I got to take a nap with the wires telling them how my brain works. We're gonna take a picture of it too."

Macy eyed Daniel for more information. "Oh wow, honey! It sounds like you had a blast with Daddy. I'm so glad. I bet you have some homework, huh?"

"Yes, I get to trace my name in cursive! I'm good at it too."

Macy laughed. "Of course you are, why don't you show me in a few minutes? Go ahead and get started. I'll be in soon.

Help yourself to some fruit for a snack. We need to get your brain reset from those donuts!" Macy laughed and scuffed Phoenix's head as he sprang into the house.

Once Phoenix was inside, Macy questioned Daniel. "He lost his balance?"

"Yeah, we had just had a pillow fight and the next thing I knew, his eyes rolled into the back of his head. He got real pale and it was like he passed out but he was still standing. I'm waiting for the neurologist to call me now."

"Daniel, why didn't you call me or text me?! Headaches are one thing, but this is—"

"Calm down, Macy. I knew you were going through a lot and I took care of it. I did everything I didn't do when he was born, okay? I was reactive, thorough…I did everything *you* would have done. I got tests done; we spent half the day in the pediatric neurologist's office."

"You still should have called me."

"Well, Macy, sometimes he's going to be with me and you're just going to have to trust my judgment. I make the decisions when I have Phoenix. You might not always agree with them and likewise, but this is the way you wanted it."

Daniel was tough with Macy. She didn't like it, but she couldn't argue with any of it. His posture softened.

"Sorry about Carl. I was closer to him than my own father. He was a hell of a good man." He reached out and touched her hand.

The gesture produced a tearful response from Macy but she pulled her hand away and turned her head.

He noticed she was no longer wearing her wedding band. "So, I guess it's really over?" Daniel asked.

"It was over when you went out to the Sky Adult Bar for some pussy. Or maybe it was the hidden accounts or credit cards…. I'll probably never know exactly when it was over."

They gazed at each other for a moment. There was pain in Daniel's eyes Macy had never seen before.

Daniel turned to leave and Macy watched him get in his car. She looked farther down the street and saw a man sitting in a car across the street from her house—it was Jakub. He wanted to see what Phoenix looked like. Macy's heart began to race even more. She couldn't believe he was there. It upset her that he didn't respect her wishes to be alone. She watched Daniel pull out of her driveway.

Macy opened her front door and yelled to Phoenix, "I'll be right there in a minute, okay baby?"

"Reminder, I'm not a baby!" Phoenix yelled back.

Macy grabbed her phone and called Jakub. "What the hell are you thinking?"

"I would assume that was your husband?"

"Yes, that was Daniel."

"And that was little Phoenix with the Spider Man backpack?" Jakub asked.

"Yes it was; why didn't you respect my wishes and give me some time?"

"I can win that little boy's heart, Macy! He's still young enough. I know I can."

Macy stood looking down the street at Jakub with the phone to her ear. She was annoyed. He disregarded her completely. "He's my child, Jakub. It will be too confusing to him. Please go back to the bed and breakfast. Don't do that again."

"As you wish, Macy. It was not my intention to upset you. I want to know all of you in every way possible. He is yours and I love everything that belongs to you."

Macy eased her hardened demeanor. "Let's talk tomorrow. He needs to be my priority tonight."

"Remember, Macy, I came back to the US to see you. I will be here when you are ready for me."

It was true. She asked him to come. She felt a pang of guilt. She was wondering if that had been an impulsive request. Daniel was a good father. The two had a special bond. She didn't like the idea that Jakub was thinking about how he was going to fit into Phoenix's life. It was too soon.

Macy went back to the house. Phoenix was hunched over his homework. He was pale and his eyes were hazy.

"Hey love bug, how's homework going?"

"Umm, I'm trying to concentrate, but I'm having a hard time."

"Well, let's see if I can help you." Macy noticed that Phoenix's hand was trembling as he wrote. "You're shaking, honey. Did you have a snack?"

"Uh-hum, I ate a banana with peanut butter. Sometimes my hands do that but I can still write fine. See, it's cursive."

"Did you tell the doctor about your hand, Phoenix?"

"Yeah, he said I have big hands for my age! At first I thought that was good, but then he said they were swollen like gigantic hands."

Macy looked closely at Phoenix's hands. She couldn't believe she had not noticed it before. Phoenix's hands were swollen to the size of a full grown man's.

27

*"Don't let yourself go
'Cause everybody cries
And everybody hurts sometimes."*
– REM

After Phoenix when to bed, Macy scoured the Internet for conditions and symptoms similar to what Phoenix was experiencing. She texted Daniel.

> Did you hear from the neurologist?

His response came quickly.

> No, I told you I'd keep you in the loop. I'll contact you as soon as I hear from the doctor.

Her fingers typed out her next question.

> Didn't they say they would call you today with the results?

Her phone buzzed again with his text.

> Yes, but maybe something went wrong with the tests. Who knows! It's a busy pediatric neurology office.

Macy thought for a moment.

Can you call them first thing in the morning
please?

Daniel's text came through:

I was planning on it.

Macy smiled, relieved, then sent her response.

Okay, thanks.

The next morning, Macy felt like she hadn't slept in a
month. After having slept with Jakub and worrying about
Phoenix all night, Macy was exhausted. She looked at herself in
the mirror. Her face looked more wrinkled, her stomach was
pooching out, and her armpits needed to be shaved. She lifted
up the blue button-up shirt she slept in and turned her hips to
the mirror. The cellulite was still there. Macy grabbed her
toothbrush and turned on the shower. She expected to hear
Phoenix any minute now. It was 7:00 AM and he was always
awake early—usually before her. She took a quick shower and
went to say good morning to Phoenix, who would likely be on
the couch watching cartoons.

Phoenix wasn't awake yet and it was now 7:20. Macy
went to his room. She gently put her face to his forehead and
kissed him. "Good morning, sleepyhead."

"Morning, Mommy."

"You can stay in bed if you don't feel good, honey. I took
the day off from work. You can hang out with me if you
want."

"No thanks, art is our special treat at school today. I don't
want to miss it."

Macy chuckled. "When I was a kid, I would have never
missed an opportunity to miss school. I'm glad you like school
so much, buddy. I'll fix you some scrambled eggs. Come to the

kitchen when you're ready. I need to talk to you about your granddaddy."

"Yummy," he said with a sleepy yawn.

Macy prepared the scrambled eggs and wondered how she was going to tell Phoenix that his grandfather had suddenly died. She asked for guidance from her angels and from her dad. "Help me find the right words," she said out loud. She padded over to the calendar. Today was the day she and Daniel were scheduled to divide their assets through their attorney in a legal separation agreement. She was due to be there at 9:00 AM. Maybe Daniel would hear from the neurologist when they were there together, she thought.

Phoenix padded into the kitchen dressed and ready for school. "Smells good, Mommy."

Macy smiled at how sweet he was. She knew other moms allowed more snacking and processed food, but Phoenix never seemed to mind the healthy foods she kept around the house. The two had breakfast together and Macy couldn't find the words to tell him about Carl, so she took him to school without a word about it.

"I love you; have a good day."

"I love you too! Bye!"

"Enjoy art today!" Macy called after waving.

He waved and walked into school. Macy sat watching him walk until the car behind her blew the horn.

When Macy got back home, she looked at her phone. Jakub had texted.

> **Good morning beautiful. When will I see my sunflower?**

Macy felt guilty. She had asked this man to travel the world for her; he obliged her wishes, and now she barely had a moment to offer him.

I'm sorry, Jakub. I have been crazy busy. Phoenix doesn't seem well. We are having some tests done that I hope to hear about today. I'm going to the attorney's office in a few minutes and then I will be free...literally and figuratively. Maybe we can have lunch?

He responded immediately.

Lunch has never sounded better. I hope Phoenix feels better.

Macy's fingers flew in typing her reply.

I do too.

Something wasn't right with Phoenix. She had known that for some time. Maybe she was in denial.

Macy blankly drove to the attorney's office. She pulled into the parking lot adjacent to the bland brick building. She looked around and was surprised when she didn't see Daniel's car there. She checked her phone to make sure she didn't miss a text or voicemail from him. There was nothing but a heart from Jakub.

She sat thinking about her night with Jakub. She had been so busy she hardly had a moment to replay their time in her head. She closed her eyes and pictured their intoxicating kisses. How stimulated they were. She felt like a teenager with a crush as she replayed their night in her head. She had not felt butterflies in a long time. She felt alive. She closed her eyes and remembered the surprise in his eyes when she used her breasts to hold his knee in a variation of pigeon pose. She wedged his knee in her cleavage and applied gentle pressure, closing the distance between his inner thigh and his chest. She stroked her hand slowly alongside his butt and drove her thumb deeply into the most tender part. She spent the next hour stretching

his body into various yoga positions. Her intuition roused
Jakub and it was obvious on his face.

Macy opened her eyes and focused on the building in
front of her. The gravity of her current situation took her
butterflies away. She was sitting in front of an attorney's office
about to sign a divorce agreement.

"Good morning! How can I help you?" The receptionist
was a little too peppy for Macy's taste.

"I'm Macy Westcott, here for—"

"Oh yes! I know!" she interrupted Macy with a jolly smile.
"Right this way. Mr. Blanchard is expecting you. Your
husband, uh, excuse me, errr…Mr. Westcott was already here
this morning. He signed all the documents. Your signature is
the only thing and your marriage is finito!"

"What?" Besides the woman's inappropriately jubilant
tone, Macy was confused. Wasn't Daniel going to try to stop
this? Wasn't he going to argue and negotiate these terms? She
had mentally prepared herself to battle him.

"Mr. Blanchard will explain everything."

She followed the receptionist to a stark room. Macy felt a
little uncomfortable in her yoga clothes following the tall
woman in a designer business suit. Macy looked down at her
Peace shirt and felt foolish. She thanked the receptionist and
took a seat.

"See you in a little bit!" the receptionist offered cheerfully
as she left.

Macy was left to her own thoughts as she waited for her
attorney. Everything about this felt bizarre. Daniel had gone
AWOL, the receptionist ate ecstasy for breakfast, the room she
was waiting in was a walk-in closet, her son was sick, her father
was dead, and her lover was waiting.

"Hi Mrs. Westcott. I'm John Blanchard." A tall, grey-
haired man closed the door behind him. His tone was much
more fitting for the occasion. Macy stood and shook his hand.

"Excuse my attire. I'm teaching a yoga class in a little while," she lied. Macy didn't have many other clothes these days. She rarely dressed in anything other than yoga clothes. She didn't play at gigs anymore so there was no reason to get dressed up or even wear makeup.

"Please sit down. I'm sure you're ready to have this day over, so I'll get straight to the process and you can stop me if you have questions."

Macy appreciated him making the weirdest day of her life less strange. "Thanks."

"So, Mrs. Westcott, Mr. Westcott made this pretty simple for us. I will be acting as your joint attorney unless you reject these terms and choose to hire someone individually. As of this moment, I am acting on your behalf as well as Mr. Westcott's. I doubt you will feel the need to hire someone because Mr. Westcott has been quite liberal. "

"He has?" Macy said, wondering if she understood the definition of the term *liberal*.

"Yes. In fact, he has gone beyond what the courts would suggest for child support and his alimony is generous."

"Are you sure you have the right Westcotts?" Macy joked in nervous laughter.

Mr. Blanchard offered a sympathetic smile as he dropped a thick file of papers in front of Macy and handed her a pen.

"So, here's the upshot: Mr. Westcott has offered you $2,500 per month in child support and $3,000 per month in alimony for the next three years. He would like to have 50/50 rights and 50/50 visitation with Phoenix. This means you will need to stay in the state with less than sixty miles distance between your homes. Against my advice, he would like to discuss these terms with you in regard to which days of the week your son is with you. I would prefer the two of you nail down specifics now, but nonetheless, he wants to work directly with you on this. Mr. Westcott has agreed to sign over the IRA in your name and half of his 401K. In addition—"

"Wait, what? I don't have an IRA or a 401K. There must be a mistake."

"No ma'am, there are copies in the file for you to see. Section 3 contains the financials, if you'd like to take a look."

"Yes, please," Macy said in disbelief.

"I'll give you a moment to look over those documents and I'll be back in a few moments," he said gently.

Macy quickly opened the file. The first page stopped her: *Termination of marriage – Daniel Westcott vs. Macy Oona Westcott.* Macy swallowed hard. Years of their marriage summed up in inkblots. Memories rolled through her head like an old movie. She remembered a happier time when there was less responsibility between them. They used to be so playful with each other. When did they stop laughing? How did it all come to this?

Macy flipped quickly to Section 3. After a few moments, she realized that once a year since they were married, there had been a deposit to an IRA with her name. Each transaction corresponded with her July birthday. Suddenly Macy felt sick. She tried to swallow but there was no saliva in her mouth.

Mr. Blanchard came back into the room holding a water bottle. "Here you go. Thought you might like some water."

"I...I...thanks for the water," Macy said as she sat back in her chair, completely dismayed. She drank the entire bottle.

"Too bad that wasn't vodka," she mumbled under her breath.

Mr. Blanchard sat down at the massive table again. It was out of proportion to the room size and almost took up every inch of the bleak space. "Mrs. Westcott, can I answer any questions for you?"

"I...I...I didn't know about these accounts Daniel had set up in my name. I...I'm just surprised he would do that. All this time...I had no idea. I thought he was so selfish and cheap and controlling and...oh my gosh."

"Ah, I see. Well, it appears to be that he was a planner."

Macy thought of Oona's words about Carl. Suddenly she felt incredible remorse. She couldn't believe Daniel had set up an account for her to be financially comfortable. Why didn't he just tell her that he was setting money aside for their retirement?

"Did he have one for himself?"

"You're not privy to that information; however, Mr. Westcott asked that you respect his privacy in regard to his PayPal and personal credit card accounts until he can sit and talk with you directly with a counselor. Further, he would like you to sign a confidentiality agreement in exchange for his generosity," Mr. Blanchard said, opening another binder. "Here you can see the entire net amount of your funds and how they were allocated to different accounts." He pointed to a sheet of charts that explained how Daniel graphed their monthly expenses.

"Here's a college fund organized for Phoenix. I'd say you're more than halfway there. There's a healthy amount saved for his tuition. My daughter is going to State and by the time she finishes, we will have paid close to $120,000!"

Macy gazed at the paper and slumped deeper into her seat. She was blindsided by Daniel's generosity. Had she been wrong about his intentions this whole time? She thought he was acting out of a need to control everything, when really he was trying to provide a way for them to enjoy retirement. Her mind was muddled. At the same time, they had thousands more than she thought was possible. Why was he so controlling over their finances?

"Why wouldn't he just share this information with me? Why act like he couldn't remember passwords?" Macy was in disbelief.

"You and your son will not have to move anytime soon. If you wish to stay in your home after the divorce, you'll be able to afford it."

The word *divorce* smacked Macy hard. They were getting divorced. Suddenly everything became real. Her life as Daniel's wife was ending. Her father was dead. Mukha was dead. She made love to someone else. She was going to be a divorcée. Macy bent over and put her head between her knees.

"Mrs. Westcott, are you okay?"

Mr. Blanchard pushed the *intercom* button on the phone. "Louise, can you bring a wet cloth in here?"

Seconds later the smiling receptionist opened the door to the abyss and clicked her tongue as she handed Mr. Blanchard a wet brown paper towel. "Here ya go! Enjoy!"

Macy was still doubled over and wanted to crawl into a ball in the corner. She logically knew this was a generous offer. She understood there would be no more pressure to clip coupons, to shop two or three different grocery stores each week in order to find the best sales. No more justifying a new sports bra. All of these thoughts should have made her feel relief. Instead, Macy lunged for the wastebasket and threw up cottage cheese and water.

Mr. Blanchard sat astonished, watching Macy. She couldn't sign the papers; she could barely stand.

"Mrs. Westcott, I understand this is an emotional ordeal. Change is never easy. But if you don't sign and initial the papers, the contract is voided," he warned.

Macy felt plagued. She grabbed her purse and stumbled, wobbling, out the door, slamming her shoulder against the doorframe, regaining her balance and erratically walking out the building to her car. Her rapid breathing caused her hands to tingle and go numb. When her face touched the fresh air, she stopped and took a deep breath. She fumbled for her keys. Scratching the paint, she inserted the key to the car door and quickly sat down. Once seated, she took slower, longer breaths. Her head rested against the steering wheel.

Suddenly a noise made her jump. It took her a moment to recognize it was her cell phone ringing.

28

"But 'happily ever after' fails
And we've been poisoned by these fairytales."
– Don Henley

"Daniel." Macy's voice was breathy. She didn't know what to say. "Daniel, I'm at the attorney's office. I didn't—"

"Macy. I'm not calling to negotiate terms of the divorce."

"But, Daniel, I didn't—"

"Damnit, Macy! This isn't about us!" Daniel exploded. "There's someone more important than us right now. I just got off the phone with the pediatric neurologist. We need to meet him in his office this afternoon."

"What's wrong with Phoenix?"

Daniel was quiet.

"Daniel. Tell me. What is wrong with my son?"

"We can't jump to conclusions just yet. They confirmed he is having simple partial seizures. They want to do an MRI right away."

"Seizures?"

"…And they are afraid the brain misfires are going to become bigger."

"Bigger?" Macy was confused.

"They think he's at risk of having a grand mal seizure because something is putting pressure on his brain."

"Jesus Christ." Macy's eyes welled up with tears.

"Let's just stay calm and talk to the doctor this afternoon. Okay? I will text you the address information. The appointment is at 3:45. Can you pick up Phoenix from school early and get him there?"

"Of course."

"See you there."

"Daniel…"

"Macy, don't…let's just focus on Phoenix right now."

Macy took a long breath and forced herself to stifle her thoughts and restrain her mouth. "Okay," she said reluctantly.

* * *

Jakub was growing restless. He could feel that something was off. He had a lot of compassion for Macy's grief over her father. He didn't want to be a burden to her. But he was here and he wanted her to take advantage of that. His visa wouldn't allow him much time. He wanted to comfort her. He wanted to be her confidant. He thought of her constantly. By 1:00 PM he knew she wasn't coming for lunch. He coped by texting her one sentence. Then he sat in the middle of the bed they made love in and began to meditate. He asked Macy's angels to bring her happiness, good health, and love. He asked her father to keep her safe and bring forth her well being above all other things.

When he came out of his meditation, Jakub had one thought.

Sometimes truly loving someone is accepting their decisions even when it isn't what you want.

He held that thought for a few moments…and then a few moments more. He had a feeling that this day was going to be pivotal for Macy, but he didn't know how. He began to feel their distance.

* * *

By 2:00 PM, Macy was fidgety to see Phoenix. She pulled up to the carpool circle outside of his school. She bustled inside and asked the office receptionist to page Phoenix. Within moments, Phoenix rounded the corner to the office.

"Mommy! What are you doing here?"

"Well, I need a date for some ice cream and I couldn't think of anyone else. So, you're it, kid," Macy said cheerfully.

"Yay!" he said and rushed into her arms.

Macy hugged Phoenix for a long time and was overcome by emotions. She pulled him tight to her chest and then put distance between them so she could really look at him. She cupped his chin with her hand. "Such a handsome date." She gazed into his tired eyes. It dawned on her that she had been so self-consumed recently she had not really looked at him. She stood motionless, not able to move as she scrutinized his angelic features. Phoenix was the best of Macy and the best of Daniel. He was resilient yet carefree, intuitive, empathic, sensitive but still spontaneous. Macy found herself treasuring this moment.

Macy stopped at an ice cream shop close to the neurology office. They splurged on double chocolate chip ice cream with Oreo topping for Macy and peanut butter, M&Ms and sprinkles for Phoenix. Macy was unusually lenient about how many toppings he added. She was playful with Phoenix, stealing a scoop of his ice cream and flicking it at his face. At 3:15, Macy told Phoenix in a nonchalant manner that they needed to look closer at his amazing brain today. Her cool and collected delivery left Phoenix unconcerned. When they arrived at the neurologist's office, Daniel was there to greet them.

"Daddy!" Phoenix ran to his father and jumped in his arms.

"Hey Scooter!" Daniel pulled out his insurance card and got them checked in. Macy felt a stab of guilt as she realized Daniel's job had always provided them the safety net of health insurance. She never had to worry about going to the doctor. It seemed that his company had such a reputable health plan; there was never an issue seeing a health provider. All these years, she had taken that for granted.

Macy and Daniel sat in the waiting room. She looked at him closely as he interacted lively with Phoenix. His hairline was receding. His skin was pale. He looked less toned today. He was slightly hunched over. Straightaway Macy felt nostalgic for him. Where had all the time gone? He was still that same man she met at the bar years ago. She thought back to a time when he adored her for her quirky and eccentric style. Back when she appreciated his straight-laced, no nonsense structure. The characteristics they once admired about each other were the same attributes driving a wedge between them. These days Daniel seemed to be annoyed that she never finished college. Back then, he appreciated that she wanted to follow her passions. How did their perceptions change so drastically? Had they grown so stubborn they could not recognize value in the other? Macy looked down at her hands. She had never noticed them before, but there were three freckles. She picked at one. The skin wasn't as taut; her pores were larger than she remembered. For a moment, she saw Oona's hands.

The nurse appeared and escorted them out double doors and into a doublewide trailer. Macy was dumbfounded when she climbed the stairs. This camper was equipped with state-of-the-art technology. In the center sat an MRI machine. Surrounding the cradle there were cameras, lights, monitors, humming electronics. Macy's mind flashed of an image of an astronaut pod. She thought of Phoenix climbing in to be launched out of orbit. She felt that everything was out of control. She caught a glimpse of herself in one of the many mirrors adhered to the wall. Macy's hair looked stringy. Her sweater was baggy and her yoga pants looked more like sweat pants that had been shrunk in the dryer. She turned her attention back to Phoenix, who was awestruck by the mobile MRI machine.

The doctor climbed in next. "Hello Mr. and Mrs. Westcott. I'm Dr. Stapleton," he said with a reassuring smile. "Phoenix!" he said over the humming of the machine. "Are you ready to take a ride in my spaceship?"

Without hesitation, Phoenix yelled, "Yeah!"

Macy and Daniel laughed at his enthusiasm. They caught each other's eye for a moment and looked away.

The doctor explained the procedure. It would be painless and boring, but if Phoenix did well, he would get to choose from a toy chest full of toys and stickers.

Phoenix climbed into the machine.

"Okay Phoenix, my machine is going to take some pictures of you, so be sure to smile, but be still, got it?"

"Got it!" Phoenix said with a great desire to be cooperative.

The technicians began the twenty-minute process of collecting images of Phoenix's brain.

"I'm sure the two of you are anxious to get this done. So, unlike adult imaging, we will be able to provide you with quick results. When the images are captured, the results will be sent to my laptop and I'll be out soon thereafter to let you know what they reveal." Dr. Stapleton turned and walked down the stairs of the camper.

The technician instructed Macy and Daniel to sit behind a thick clear wall. They would be able to see Phoenix the whole time and with the click of a button, they would be able to speak into a microphone where he would be able to hear their voices.

The technician pressed the button and spoke, "Okay this is ground control to Captain Phoenix."

Phoenix laughed, "Arrg! This is Captain P at your service," Phoenix said with a pirate's accent. Daniel and Macy laughed.

The technician continued, "When we start, the bed will slide you into my cool space pod. You'll hear a loud buzzing noise. That's normal. It's just my machine taking pictures, okay? It's really important that you be as still as you can. I'll pass the mic over to your mom and dad and get started."

Phoenix grew slightly nervous when the instructions were given. "Mom?"

"I'm here, honey!" Macy said, but she forgot to push the microphone button.

Daniel pushed the button and motioned for her to calm down and say it again.

"I'm here, Captain," she said steadily this time.

29

"I would love to be your lonely neighbor
The kind who asks you for a little sugar
You invite me in, grab the coffee from the tin
I want you now more than I did."
– Oh Honey

After the MRI was completed, Macy, Daniel, and Phoenix went back to the pediatric waiting room. Macy took the time during the transition to check her phone. She saw a text from Jakub.

> Whatever is keeping you from me, although I hope it is not your feelings, I understand. I miss you, my sunflower. I am here when you are ready to turn to me.

Butterflies fluttered in her stomach. She felt horrible. It was rash and thoughtless to involve him in her wreck of a life. What was she thinking asking him to come here? How could she have been so quick to make love to him? How could she regret something so organic and pure? The gravity of the situation slammed into her. *What have I done?*

For so long, Macy had beat the drum of what Daniel wasn't doing right that she hadn't been able to notice what he *was* doing right. She was so focused on what he lacked that she couldn't see all the positives he possessed. Over the years, her perception had become skewed. Now that she was free to be on the outside looking in, she was beginning to comprehend things differently. She imagined another woman sitting in the waiting room with Daniel, comforting them. She felt an intense agony envelop her.

Macy looked up from her phone and caught Daniel staring at her. The look in his eye was pleading, as if his eyebrows were imploring her to come to her senses. Macy quickly looked down at her hands. She was no longer wearing her wedding ring. She looked at Daniel's ring finger. He had still not taken his band off. Macy's mind was tormented with questions. After learning that Daniel made painstakingly difficult efforts to afford their future together, what else was she wrong about? How could he have slept with another woman and caused this slippery slope of events? It had all come undone. It was too late to nullify the mistakes and pain. Everything was spiraling downward.

Macy felt heavy in her chair but turned her attention back to Phoenix. She was grateful there were toys to keep him occupied. He found an Etch-a-Sketch in the trunk of toys. As if they both realized he was playing with it at the same time, Macy and Daniel both exclaimed simultaneously, "Hey, an Etch-a-Sketch! I haven't seen one of those in years!"

Daniel looked at Macy, his expression pained. "Jinx," he said flatly.

The nurse came out and explained that Daniel and Macy would meet with the doctor in a consultation room to review the results of the MRI. Her role as nurse now became that of a babysitter. "Phoenix and I will have a great time etching things, won't we?"

Phoenix was so enthralled in his creation that his "Yes ma'am" was barely audible.

"Clearly you don't feel comfortable with this, Phoenix," Macy joked.

Phoenix was used to his mother's sarcastic humor. He snickered under his breath.

Daniel held the door open for Macy and placed his hand on the small of her back. Macy was surprised at the surge that went through her body at this small gesture. He followed her into the consultation room and sat next to her waiting for the doctor. The walls were a warm blue, adorned with paintings generic enough to be appropriate. There was a small desk facing two burgundy leather armchairs.

The two sat in silence for several minutes. "Wonder where the doctor is," Macy murmured.

Daniel didn't respond. Another soundless moment passed.

Daniel finally spoke. "It's not appropriate to talk about it now, but assuming you found the terms of the divorce to be satisfactory, we will need to discuss Phoenix's custody schedule. I thought we could handle that part without the attorney."

There were so many things Macy wanted to say. "Daniel, I didn't—"

Dr. Stapleton opened the door to the tiny office. He slung a folder across the desk and flopped into his big wingback chair.

"There's no easy way to say this, folks."

Macy stared hard at the doctor, contracting every muscle in her abdominals as if she were about to receive a blow to the stomach.

"Phoenix is expressing gigantism in his hands. I'm sure you've noticed the size of his hands is quite large for his age. This is a result of an overactive pituitary gland secreting too much growth hormone. The reason this symptom is of concern, aside from the obvious, is because it's usually caused by an adenoma."

"What is that?" Macy interrupted.

"Mr. and Mrs. Westcott, Phoenix has a tumor."

"*What?!*" Macy exclaimed.

The doctor continued, "The mass is measuring 4.8 millimeters. It's creating pressure on the tissues surrounding the pituitary gland. This is why Phoenix is experiencing hand tremors and headaches. It's a very serious situation."

"Holy shit," Daniel said under his breath.

The doctor went on, "We have two options. Option one is called transsphenoidal surgery. This means we will go through the nose to extract the tumor. Because of the complex nature of the procedure, we would form a team of doctors who have experience with this from UNC as well as Duke."

"What's the other option?" Daniel asked.

Dr. Stapleton answered, "It's basically radiation. It's called Gamma Knife radiosurgery, or stereotactic radiosurgery. It can deliver a high dose of radiation to the tumor cells in a single dose while limiting the amount of radiation to the normal surrounding tissues. Duke is one of the few facilities where this procedure is available in the US. This type of radiation may bring growth hormone levels back to normal within three to five years, but follow-up care will last the rest of his life. Either way, we are in for a long process here. I would encourage you to take the results and get second and third opinions, but do so quickly."

Macy was glaring at Dr. Stapleton. She hated him. She hated the sound of his voice. She hated his bald head and puffy wingback chair. A fire grew in the cavity of her gut. She felt like she was reliving Phoenix's birth. She felt like she was going to have to will her son to live all over again.

"This is BULLSHIT." Macy slammed her hand on to the doctor's mahogany desk and knocked over a container of pens. "I want a second opinion." She turned around and looked at Daniel, whose color had drained from his normally warm face.

Daniel ignored Macy and held his gaze to the doctor. "You already got a second opinion, didn't you?" Daniel asked. His voice quivered as he spoke. Macy was surprised at his intuition. He had been the calm, keen one still using his wits while Macy's fight or flight response swallowed her whole.

"Yes. That's what took me so long. I had my suspicions earlier on and reached out to a colleague from Johns Hopkins who agreed to look over Phoenix's results real time. He concurs with my diagnosis, but of course you are welcome to consult with anyone you wish."

Macy felt like she had received a strike to the stomach.

"Damnit!" Macy yelled.

"Macy, stop it! When are you going to learn to deal with difficult situations without blowing up?" Daniel said vehemently. "When Phoenix was born, I didn't react the way you thought I should. In fact, you've never let me live it down. But you're not going to make Phoenix better by throwing a childish fit. Sometimes less is more. I'm sure you yoga people have a term for that. Now, I want you to sit down and compose yourself." His voice was forceful and demanding. He was the voice of reason way back in Macy's head that she could not hear. She sat hard on the edge of her seat and stared straight ahead.

Daniel turned to Dr. Stapleton. "What are the risks of the radio surgery?" he asked.

Dr. Stapleton looked at the two empathetically. Macy was not able to speak. She felt like a child with no words. She wanted to stomp her feet and throw a temper tantrum until this whole situation went away.

"Good question." The doctor continued in a softer tone, "Swelling in the brain tissues may occur—it usually goes away without treatment. But some people may need medicine to control this swelling and sometimes an incision is necessary to treat the brain swelling caused by the radiation. But if all goes well, Phoenix would be able to go home that same day."

"I guess Macy and I have a lot of research to do." Daniel's calm assertiveness came through again. Macy took notice of how much he was able to accomplish by keeping his cool.

The doctor spoke again. "I understand. I hate to add pressure to an already difficult situation, but I would recommend that you try to make a decision as quickly as possible. There will be a lot of moving parts involved in his treatment and the pressure on his brain is concerning."

Macy finally cracked. It came in waves. Her snivel became a whimper. Her whimper grew into a sob until her sobs gave way to a wail. She was inconsolably distraught. Daniel felt inclined to offer her the solace of his arms but resisted. Instead, he stood and shook Dr. Stapleton's hand.

"Thank you for your thorough explanation and time. We will let you know as soon as possible."

"Of course," the doctor said.

Daniel turned to Macy. "Macy, it's late. Why don't I take Phoenix home with me tonight?"

"No!" she protested through her tears.

Daniel was firm. "Macy, you need time to get yourself together. I don't want him to see your reaction right now and freak out. I know you don't want that either. Let's sleep on things. Come over in the morning and we will make a decision together."

Daniel seemed taller and more confident than he was just an hour ago. Macy relented. "Fine." She sniffled.

Daniel turned to the door. "Don't let him see you like this," Daniel warned her again, not making eye contact with her.

Macy put her head in her hands and Daniel walked back to the pediatric waiting room. "Hey scooter!" She could hear his voice through the door.

Daniel put on a brave front for Phoenix though his stomach was thrashing. He wondered how his life came to this. He thought he had done all the right things for his family. He had been responsible. He had done all the things the breadwinner and good father was supposed to do. Yet, he was losing his wife. He was mourning the loss of a man he had great admiration for. He had gotten involved with a woman he didn't care for. His son had a brain tumor. Daniel felt frayed at the edges.

30

"I had the strangest feeling
Your world's not all it seems
So tired of misconceiving
What else this could've been."
— Mumford & Sons

Macy sat in the doctor's office for a long time. Eventually, she made her way to the parking lot. She saw the ice cream shop where she and Phoenix had enjoyed cones early that day. It seemed so long ago.

She sat in the front driver's seat for a long time. She felt desperate, fragmented, shattered.

Her fingers flew over her phone's keyboard in a text message to Jakub.

I'm coming undone.

In seconds his response came, as if he had written it long ago and was waiting to respond to her splintered cry. His response was a quote by Cynthia Occelli:

> For a seed to reach its greatest expression, it must come completely undone. The shell cracks, its insides come out and everything changes. To someone who doesn't understand growth, it would look like complete destruction.

Night pulled the shade over the last of the day and low fog covered the ground. On the way home, the rain smacked against the windows with a fierce vengeance. It echoed like fingernails rapping desperately for hope. Macy's windshield wipers screeched. Condensation collected and dripped down the glass, a reflection of her soul's cry.

Macy squinted at the pellets slicing through the air sideways. The daunting lightning illuminated the sky. For a brief moment it looked like a snapshot of daytime. The roaring thunder was deafening. No matter how many times she prepared for it, the piercing boom jolted her. She felt a crater develop inside the length of her sternum. Her heartbeat was almost audible. The gravity of her situation pulled her with a powerful undertow.

Macy pulled into her driveway. She opened the car door, took several steps forward directly into the storm, and stood in a puddle of self-loathing. Her gaze became blurry as she stared into oblivion. She hated herself for losing her identity in her marriage, for stuffing away her musical talents, for not trusting her instincts more, for not going to more counseling, for not being a better mother and wife, for being selfish, for feeding her soul to another man, for having an insatiable appetite to be with him...for the pain her very existence was now causing him. Her heart rate spiked. She was the epitome of all that she despised.

Her fingernails dug deep into her skin, toughened by her own self-hatred. "Fuck!" The word exploded like a firework off her tongue.

A gust of wind whipped around her, lifting her hair from her shoulders, exposing her long neck. Her shirt rippled in the blast, tugging against her skin like a tattered sail in the night's current. Rain assaulted her face. She knew she deserved this pain. All of it.

She thought of ways to end her intense pain. She wanted to die.

The ground roared, vibrating thunder under her feet. For moments her sobs had no sound.

Lightning cracked through the sky as Macy stretched her fingers wide, her palms facing the heavens. She stood like a crucifix. Tears streamed down her face.

"Give me the tumor. I'm the one who deserves it. You fucking coward. They call you God? Then, take my life. I don't want it."

Her voice shook and broke off as she took in a sharp breath. Her angry rant became a plea.

"Please God, be a thief in this night—take me away!"

31

"I lie in the dead of night and I wonder
Whose covers you're between
And it's sad laying in his bed
You feel hollow, so you crawl home back to me."
– Plain White T's

The last thing Macy remembered, she was outside. Somehow she was now inside her home neatly wrapped up in a fleece blanket she didn't recognize. There was a cup of hot water with a steeping tea bag beside her. The hues released from the trapped herbs swirled to the surface of the water. Next to the cup of tea were a sunflower and a handwritten note.

My dearest Macy. In one glance, I saw the depths of your soul and left you nowhere to hide. Like a blind man seeing the sun for the first time, your beauty caused me to buckle. I love you completely without pride. The first time I heard your voice in the yoga studio, I knew I would die with your song on my heart. The greatest tragedy I have ever known is falling in love with the right woman at exactly the wrong time. It is a travesty that our love story will come to this blunt ending. The universe has played a sinister joke on us. And still I find myself thankful to have had some of you rather than nothing at all. No one is to blame.

You gave me immeasurable joy—more than I have ever tasted in lifetimes preceding this one. I will carry you in the four chambers of my heart always. Oh how I will always wish to bathe you in sunflowers. You are a lion to those who see you but your insides are that of a delicate butterfly. How can I justify causing you more pain? I cannot. I will leave the US tomorrow night. But I will offer one prayer every day for the rest of my life. I will ask God this: to please deliver us the next lifetime together.

You are not my soulmate, Em. You are my twin flame. We are from the same soul. I know this to be true. And I know you do too. When

you are sad, be still. Know I am in the wind that kisses your neck. When
you dream, I will whisper your name through the petals of the sunflowers.
You own my heart for all of eternity.

    ~ Jakub

Macy pressed the letter to her heart. She lifted the fleece blanket to her nose and sniffed. There it was, as she knew it would be—the scent of home. She thought of her old tapestry. The smell of it and the butterfly that sat on the elephant's nose. She closed her eyes just in time for the tears to cascade down her cheeks. She knew she would never see Jakub again. Not in this lifetime.

She kept her eyes closed the rest of the night.

Macy's dreams were vivid. She could hear the beating of a gavel, and then a discussion ensued. The light was too bright to see anything. Voices were vying about her soulmate and her twin flame. The council was divided.

Suddenly it was night again and Macy was back out in the rain. She ran. Her arms pumped, her breath a cloud, the ground a treadmill. Thunder clapped as loudly as her heart. She was a warrior running through the elements, telepathically yelling to Jakub. *"Don't leave!"* She sprinted; her heart was an erratic cadence.

She saw the magnolia tree, and beside it, the inn. She stopped, put her hands on her legs, and bent over to catch her breath. Phoenix flashed in her mind.

A noise rose above the dimming rain. At first she thought it was lightning—then she heard the engine, the tires slapping through the water.

She quickly shuffled off the street. The car passed. She had been so hasty running in the street in the dark night. She shook her head. What had gotten into her? How could she walk away? She realized she couldn't have it all. Not right now, anyway. She slowly turned and walked away from the inn.

The sun sliced through her living room blinds in the morning. Macy cracked her heavy eyes. The way the sun severed the room conjured up thoughts of a light saber. Phoenix loved Star Wars. A wave of sadness washed over her.

Macy's bones felt brittle from sleeping in one position the entire night. It took her a few minutes to unwrap herself from the fleece blanket. She slowly stood up; it was painful to straighten her joints. She looked at the clock—7:00 AM. She furrowed her brow and bit her tongue deep in concentration. She had to get moving.

The blanket had fallen to the floor. She picked it up like she was handling a valuable timepiece, then held it to her nose and folded it neatly and placed it in her trunk with her tapestry. She started to close the old box, but she stopped. She reached in and fingered the tapestry, inundated with memories of a time when she was young, carefree, open, light, frisky, fun…all the things she wasn't now. She sighed, stretching her body, and heard her bones snap and pop.

Macy arrived at Daniel's later that morning. Before her third knock, Daniel yanked open the door. He stood in a gray thermal shirt and drawstring pants Macy had not seen before. The shirt was snug around his biceps and Macy realized she had not noticed his stature in quite some time. His frame was sturdy and muscular. She had been so concerned about her own figure on the cruise that she hadn't taken the time to notice his build. She wondered in what other ways was she narcissistic. Daniel had matured into a handsome man. They were different people than they were a decade ago. She studied him.

"Hi," he said quietly as he opened the door wider for her to step inside.

"Hi." She shyly diverted her eyes to the floor.

"Come in. We have a lot to discuss, so I let Phoenix go to school, but I'd like to pick him up early, assuming we can come to an agreement." He motioned to his kitchen table, where Macy sat. "I took the liberty of making you some green tea." He handed her a steaming mug.

Macy was taken back by this gesture of kindness. "Wow, um, thank you."

"No problem."

She sipped as he began to talk. Distracted by the fact he had prepared her tea with exactly the right amount of agave and lemon zest, she smiled coyly, lost her concentration.

"What? Do I have toothpaste on my chin?"

Macy looked up. Daniel was staring at her.

"No, sorry. Thanks for the tea. It's perfect."

"You're welcome. So, I thought first we should discuss the options for dealing with the tumor." Daniel was uncomfortable saying the word *tumor*. Hearing it made Macy's skin crawl. Her son had a brain tumor.

"Okay."

Daniel went on, "Then, I thought we should discuss custody and…Macy?"

Macy's mind had floated away again. "Sorry." She started looking around at Daniel's place. She had never been inside before. Framed photos lined the wall. Macy took one of the pictures of Daniel and Phoenix. "Nice photos." She motioned to the wall. They were blown up, matted and framed nicely. There were some recent ones she had never seen. Apart from the photos, everything was in order. Minimalistic. Phoenix's toys were neatly stacked in labeled bins. Macy thought of the words Daniel used the day before.

"Aparigraha," she said out loud.

"What?" Daniel questioned.

"It's the term for less is more. You're right, we yoga people have a word for it." Daniel was a single father in this home raising his only son. He had moved on. He was keeping things in simple order.

Macy noticed a woman's jacket hanging on the coat rack beside the kitchen door.

"Macy? Are you going to be able to have this discussion today?" Daniel pressed.

"What? Oh. Yes, sorry. I've just never really been inside your place."

Daniel looked around. "I guess not. Well, this is my house. Well, not my house. But, my uh, home away from home. Sorta...." His voice trailed off.

"I see why Phoenix likes it here. It's comfortable." She nodded slowly.

"It works for now. After we finalize the divorce, I would like to get something more permanent."

There was an awkward silence between them. After a long pause, Macy started first.

"I didn't sign the divorce papers."

"What?!" Daniel said in a booming voice. "Geez Macy, what else could you want? I made sure you don't have to work for the next eight to ten years. All I want is 50/50 time with my son! Is that too much to ask?" The bass in his voice was thundering. Macy shuddered.

"It's not that, Daniel."

"Well, what the hell is it?"

Something was stirring inside Macy—an awakening. Macy was confused by the contention in her soul. On one hand she wanted to run to Daniel and wrap her arms around him. She wanted things to be the way they used to be. She stood looking at him in his kitchen. *His kitchen.* None of it was right.

A dormant passion ignited inside her. This wasn't the way it was supposed to be. They were a family. But on the other hand, there was a crusade running commentary in her head. A woman's jacket was hanging up in his home. Anger boiled up in Macy's throat.

"Why did you do it?" she shouted, surprising even herself.

Confusion covered Daniel's face. "Why did I do what?"

"Why the women on PayPal? Why the condom? Why did you have sex with some bimbo at a strip bar when we were supposed to be working on our marriage?"

"I told you, Macy, it was locker room talk. I want to talk about it with your counselor."

"You expect me to believe nothing happened? Your hand was down a woman's G-string. And now a woman's jacket is hanging in your house? And you expect me to believe nothing happened." Anger overcame her just as it did when she first discovered the photograph.

Daniel looked over his shoulder and saw the coat. He blushed.

"I didn't say *nothing* happened. We were on different wavelengths for a long time, Macy. You went to bed early, I stayed up late. You always had your head up some guru's ass learning about some metaphysical bullshit. You're always meditating or playing guitar. I don't know what my passion is or what my legacy will be. You were always bigger than life, Macy. Everyone knows you for being so talented. I don't have a burning purpose in life. It's always made me feel like we were in competition and I'm the failure because I don't have it figured out. And hell yeah, it was nice to get some attention. It was nice to feel like someone actually saw me as a man with positive qualities." He continued, "I got addicted to it. Relationships are fun when they're new. There's no stress. No bullshit. They always think I'm brilliant in the beginning. Things aren't so heavy." He looked at her seriously. "Don't act like this is all my fault. You just gave up on us. You just walked away. But that's the typical Macy. If you don't like something, it's expendable. So, you know what? Yes, I hooked up with someone at Sky Adult Bar."

Macy was in shock.

"But I didn't have sex with her," he went on. "I ended up talking to her for hours about my childhood. We kissed goodbye and that was it. Sometimes I pay for women to meet me when I travel. I just like their company. It's easier to talk to them than it is you. I never wanted to disappoint you. I talk to them about my upbringing a lot. I don't know why. I'm fucked up, I guess. I like for them to hit on me, talk to me like I'm interesting, exciting, new. But I never have sex with them. I never had sex with anyone until you accused me of screwing some bimbo. Then I figured, why the hell not? She thinks I did anyway. So why not? So, I did. I had sex with someone else."

This was all too much truth for Macy but she couldn't help but to torture herself more. "Well, when? And who did you have sex with?"

He hesitated as if he was chewing on brick pavers.

"We should really talk about this with your counselor," Daniel said. "I'm telling you, Macy, I'm fucked up in the head. Even I don't know who I am. All I know is that you made it clear I should move on. My parents were here with Phoenix. So, after my company launch party, I went out with Jesse."

Macy gasped. *Jesse.*

He continued. "Now you know. That's her jacket," he said, pointing to the coat hanger.

"Jesse?! You screwed Jesse?! I *knew* it!" Macy threw her cup of tea across the room. It smashed against the wall.

Daniel threw his hands up. "What was I supposed to do? Be celibate for the rest of my life? You had washed your hands of me and said it was over. You are impetuously hasty in your decisions and reckless with other people's feelings. In fact, for someone so 'grounded,' you act pretty immature."

He got quiet. His words hung in the air.

He began again in a softer tone. "I regret having sex with her. I was drunk and blew off steam. I wish I could take it back. I wish I could take everything back. I picked on you the way my mom picked on me. I know I need help." Daniel was referring to his controlling habits, to his constant belittling of Macy's capabilities, to hooking up the bar, but mostly he was referring to sex with Jesse. "Something changed between us, Macy. Life changed us. Everything got so heavy after Phoenix was born. We never laughed anymore. It was like my childhood all over again." His tone was somber.

Macy couldn't believe what she was hearing. She was trying to understand what had happened that night she saw the text. Had she been mistaken? Had she really misinterpreted the text? Was it really locker room talk? Had she pushed him into the arms of another woman? Was he really blaming his parents for his behaviors? Why had she been so quick to separate? Who was this man in front of her? Did she have a fight or flight response? She hated how well he knew her and that he was calling her out on the qualities she detested most about herself. Why had she not invested in more counseling to find out? Had Jakub been in the back of her mind the whole time? Did his kiss affect how she was behaving in her marriage? Was she to blame for its demise? Was Jakub? Was Daniel? Was Jesse? She calculated the timeline in her head. She and Jakub were together the same night as Daniel and Jesse. She felt sick.

Daniel and Macy sat in silence until she broke it.

"I did try to initiate closeness with you. You cope with video games and devote more attention to devices than to me. I even tried on the cruise but you were being a spoiled brat. Were you getting a lap dance in the VIP room? It wouldn't surprise me, since you couldn't even get it up for me anymore. All this time you made me feel guilty for a new pair of shoes and you were blowing hundreds on the company of whores because they made you feel important?! You've got to be fucking kidding me."

The words hurt, but they needed to be said. It was the fight that Daniel and Macy needed to have for months.

"Well, now you know how irresponsible I was being with our finances, don't you? I was trying to secure Phoenix's college tuition. Doesn't that count for something? Every time I spent money on an escort, I made a deposit into an account for you," Daniel spat.

"Is that supposed to make it all better?" she countered.

"Macy, when I was a kid, my mom blew through our family's savings account and put us into bankruptcy. My dad had no idea until it was too late. It's a humiliating family secret and yes, I screwed up, but my intentions were not evil. Hell, one of the things I love most about you is that you're not materialistic. I trusted you, I just…ugh, I don't know. I wish I could take it all back." He put his head in his palms.

Macy was shocked to hear this news. Both fell quiet. Macy thought about how Mrs. Westcott flaunted her wealth. It was just a desperate act to overcompensate for her insecurities. She felt a pang of compassion for Daniel, for his childhood. She wanted to lean across the table and take his hand but she knew too much had happened for the two of them to reconcile now. They had both broken their marriage. She had slept with another man—even more importantly, she felt her soul move because of this man. She knew the passion she felt with Jakub would have even been unsustainable. She wondered if Daniel shared that same intensity with Jesse. For some reason she believed him about the other women. Then she wondered if sex with someone new just feels temporarily thrilling. In a strange way, she was relieved they had both slept with other people. Like the guilt could be smeared evenly across the surface.

Daniel blew air audibly through his lips. After a few moments, Daniel spoke softly under his breath. "Maybe I was foolish thinking we could sort through the custody arrangements. I'll call Blanchard tomorrow and we can negotiate the rest of the terms through him."

Daniel looked defeated. He sat down in the chair across from Macy's and put his head in his hands, rubbing his eyes. He looked hollow.

Macy looked at the clock on the stove. It was 10:00 AM. She knew Jakub was packing for his flight to go home. She thought about the events that had transpired before she had reached out to him. She realized how impetuous she was to make snap judgments. She inhaled a long, expansive breath. She looked at the man sitting across from her looking strained and filled with trepidation and angst. He was a stranger, she knew. She hated herself for her role in causing this situation. She hated him for his part in it. Part of Macy wanted to run out the door and tell Jakub not to leave. But she recognized truth in many of Daniel's words. She acted first and thought later, no matter the consequences.

Macy reached in her purse and pulled out some action figures she brought for Phoenix. One of them was a little green Yoda. She fumbled with Yoda and moved his arms around. For some reason it was easier to talk when her fingers were able to fidget with something tactile.

Hesitantly Daniel asked, "So, why didn't you sign the divorce papers?"

Macy tried to define the look in Daniel's eyes. If she didn't know better, she would have mistaken it for the look of fear mixed with hope.

"Daniel, I…didn't you trust me? Why didn't you trust me enough to tell me about your mom? You confided in escorts before your own wife! Do you know how that makes me feel?"

Daniel was quiet for a long time. "Sometimes it's easier to talk to a stranger than someone you know intimately. I didn't want you to see all of my hideous imperfections. In hindsight I would have done things differently, Macy." Tears welled up in his eyes. Macy didn't know if he was emotional because of them or because of Phoenix or both. He continued, "I was a miser. I treated you like a child. I wish I hadn't been so hard on you…on me, on us. I was narcissistic. I wanted attention and got it from the wrong places. I swear to God, Macy, you can call each of the women. I never had sex with any of them—just Jesse—and I regret that terribly. It was awful and when it was over I just wanted to kill myself. My parents are fucked up and I'm no better. I need professional help. Now all of this with Phoenix…." His tone was somber and remorseful. His eyes were contrite.

They stared at each other for a long time. Macy wondered how long it had been since she looked—really looked—into Daniel's eyes. She didn't remember the last time he looked at her and didn't immediately look away.

"Well…I'm glad you were depositing money into an account for me. Looks like we're going to need it for Phoenix. Our deductible is $4,000."

"That money is yours to keep, Macy."

She laughed. "I never cared about driving a nice car or keeping up with the Joneses. You know that. I just wanted to be part of our team…to feel like I was making a contribution. Ugh…." She let out an audible exhale. She felt a sense of responsibility to Daniel's well being. She could imagine him being suicidal.

There was an interlude of silence before she spoke again. "I would trade it all to have Phoenix healthy." Her hushed tone was mournful.

Daniel knew Macy's love for Phoenix was the paragon of maternal. He knew she would give her life for Phoenix. Her voice was somber; her complexion dulled. She was far away from the animated lively woman who abducted his heart years ago. Daniel looked at the dejected woman in his kitchen. He knew he had broken her spirit. He wondered how many of the lines had he etched on her face. She was still so beautiful to him. She dignified the aging process. It struck him that he had not looked at her face in a long time. For a moment, he realized he had been trying to escape his own reality to relive a moment of his youth. A chance to shake off the mundane, to abscond the middle of their lives. Now both had made a sizeable catastrophe of their realities.

"I'm done with attorneys," Macy said as she stood from the table. She walked to clean the cup she had broken.

"That's the best thing I've heard today," Daniel said behind her. "I really think we can get through this, Macy."

Macy froze. At first she thought he was talking about their marriage. She was surprised at how much hope filled her chest. Like the embers had been fanned. Then she realized he was talking about the divorce, and about Phoenix.

"He's a tough kid," Daniel continued.

Hope escaped through her exhale. She continued wiping the mess. She threw away the shards and sat back down across from Daniel.

"Do you have a feeling which procedure would be best for Phoenix?" she asked.

"Yes."

"On the count of three?" she asked nervously.

"Okay, on the count of three."

"One…two…three…"

"Gamma knife," they both answered.

When Phoenix got home from school, Daniel and Macy delicately explained what was going on. Phoenix was unusually quiet. He only asked one thing about the surgery.

"Are they going to shave my head?"

"I don't think they're going to have to do that," Macy answered.

"It's pretty cool that the doctors can do that kind of surgery without even slicing me open," Phoenix said. "So does this mean I can have anything I want for dinner?"

Daniel and Macy laughed. "Anything you want."

"Can we play Monopoly together and order a pizza?"

Daniel looked at Macy, who smiled gently. "The greasiest, cheesiest one we can find."

The three went back to their family home and started their evening together. Laugher filled the walls when Macy chose the iron to represent her place in the game. Daniel teased that it was the first time he ever saw her use an iron. He held Macy's eyes long after the laughter stopped. She broke his gaze and looked out the window, then at the clock. The sun was down. She knew Jakub was gone. She wondered if he took part of her heart with him.

32

"When the road gets dark
And you can no longer see
Just let my love throw a spark
An' have a little faith in me."
— John Hiatt

The date was set for Phoenix's surgery. The next two weeks were a blur as the family prepared for the surgery. As instructed, the night before, Daniel and Macy made sure Phoenix didn't eat anything. They distracted him by cuddling in the master bed. It was the first time Daniel and Macy had been in their bedroom together in months. The initial awkwardness subsided as they took turns reading Phoenix story after story. They snuggled closely and Macy realized how many times Daniel had told the bedtime stories. As he rambled through the tongue twisters of *The Cat in The Hat*, she realized how much he authentically enjoyed it.

One of the stories, *Love You Forever*, was Macy's favorite. It was a story with illustrations about a mother and son throughout the span of their lives. First her baby boy became her toddler, who became her teenager, who left the home, then became a young man and married. The mother always rocked her son when he was little. As he got older, she snuck in his room and rocked him. He would always be her baby. When the young man became an adult, the mother became a very old lady. The roles reversed and the son rocked the mother—for she would always be his mommy.

Macy had read the story hundreds of times. She had never thought about where the book came from, but tonight she noticed the inscription: *Thank you for being this kind of mother to Phoenix. Love, Daniel.*

Macy read the story and became emotional, unable to speak through her tears. Daniel took her hand and squeezed gently. He gave her a reassuring look that everything was going to be alright. He took the book and finished it, choking back his tears. They were all keenly aware of the impermanence of life on this night. The three fell asleep together.

At the hospital the next morning, the staff moved swiftly as they prepared an IV delivering fluid to keep Phoenix hydrated. Next, a dye was injected to highlight his blood circulation. He was scared but followed directions. Macy and Daniel were given a choice to anesthetize Phoenix or give him four numbing shots in his scalp. Because the Gamma knife was a mechanical contraption that fit over his head like medieval head armor, Daniel and Macy opted to anesthetize him.

The day's emotions fluctuated like a yo-yo. The procedure took most of the day. The team of skilled doctors and nurses met for several hours planning the appropriate areas to treat, dosages of radiation, and how to focus the radiation beams to treat the areas. Everything was to be executed with great care and precision.

The group in charge of Phoenix's surgery was made up of radiation oncologists, world-renowned neurologists, radiation therapists, and of course Dr. Stapleton. Although Macy was confident in the team's proficiency, she was bombarded with memories of Phoenix's birth. No only did she recognize that even the most skilled expert can make mistakes; she was repulsed by the sounds and smells of a hospital. It provoked a sickening abhorrence within her gut.

Daniel studied Macy's face and knew what she was thinking. The two sat in a small waiting room outfitted with a Keurig and *People* magazines. She looked at the happy couple gracing the cover and the lightning bolt between them indicating they were splitting up because of their nanny.

Macy put her head in her hands. Daniel sat down beside her and placed his hand on her back. His touch felt natural.

She was grateful to have him go through this process with her. She put her hand on his knee.

A man from another waiting area came scuttling through the doors. Macy jumped at his presence. He eyed Macy and Daniel as he leaned against the counter with the coffee machine. He started to whistle while he placed a K-cup in the pod and pressed the brew button. He flicked a package of Equal several times before tearing it open. The machine gurgled discernibly louder before it spit hot coffee into the paper cup. Small noises seemed amplified in this antiseptic space where things were colorless, odorless, and soulless.

Macy looked more closely at the man now. He resembled Mr. Bean with his loud expressions. The man vigorously shook a carton of half & half. The jiggle of his body broke the sound of his melody just as Macy was beginning to recognize the tune. Mr. Bean removed the brewed cup and gushed creamer into it. He slurped a nip of the steaming beverage and cleared his throat in a resounding hack. As he walked out the door, he began his melody again.

Relief swept over them when Dr. Stapleton emerged from the room with a poised authoritative look. He didn't hesitate. "Phoenix did great. I'm confident we targeted and treated the tumor in its entirety."

Daniel and Macy sighed with relief and hugged each other for much longer than was customary. Both of them fell into tears. Macy's teardrops pressed into Daniel's chest. They swayed back and forth, arms encased around each other for a long time.

Dr. Stapleton quietly said, "You can go into recovery anytime now. We will be rolling him down shortly."

The two never looked up or detached.

"Macy, I'm a better man when we're together," Daniel murmured into her hair. "I love you. I don't want us to be apart. I'm glad you didn't sign the papers." He took her face in his hands. "We can work this out. You're the only woman I've ever loved. I know I screwed up...."

Macy was crying even harder now. "You're not the only one who screwed up, but it's too late. I don't know if you'll feel the same after you learn what I've done...and I don't know if I can forget it or even want to."

Daniel didn't understand her confession, but he hushed her voice with his mouth. They shared a lingering kiss. When they broke away, he looked her deeply in the eyes. "Can you still love me?"

"I have always loved you, Daniel. I never stopped. It just changed."

"We've been through so much. I don't think enough has happened to destroy our bond. It's a bond we're continuing to grow. We're a family. I believe we can work this out. Will you try? For me and Phoenix?" he pleaded. "I will be fully transparent. You can have access to my cell phone, the accounts and all the passwords. I want to be accountable to you."

She had never seen him so desperate with ambition. "I'm not sure you will want to rebuild a life with me, Daniel. I did something...I felt something for someone else that I—"

"Macy," he interrupted, "we both did things and felt things we can't change. I'm telling you—I want us to be a family again. I'm ready to be the man you need. We need each other now more than ever. Don't you see? Things go to shit when we're apart. I can get past anything if you say you're in. Just say you're in."

Macy looked into Daniel's expectant eyes. Feelings whirled around her gut. The adrenaline from Phoenix's surgery made her lightheaded. How would it feel to be with Daniel again? Would she think of Jesse every time they made love? What would she do if Jakub ever came back to the US? Could they rebuild their relationship? What about finances? What about trust?

As if he knew her doubts, he pressed on. "I'm willing to cut off all ties with Jesse. I've learned from this, Macy. I'll do things differently. We can be a team. We can wipe the slate clean. Give our family another chance. Please. Just say you're in."

For a split second Macy thought he was saying these things because he would be better off financially because he had been so generous in the offering of his divorce settlement. Then seeing the sincerity in his eyes, she chastised herself for considering such a thought. There was a hint of optimism behind his lashes.

Macy's mind played the movie of their lives together. They had experienced extreme ups and downs. Maybe they could move beyond the past and start over. She thought of her feelings for Jakub and how they had developed so quickly. Perhaps that was infatuation. Yet, she felt like she had known him forever and longer. She knew she would grieve to let him go, but here was Daniel, who she had so much love for and history with, who was finally ready to be the man she needed him to be. And a child whose life would be affected by this diagnosis forever. She was so grateful that the prognosis was positive, but helping Phoenix through this process would be a lifetime commitment.

She wondered how Daniel would react when she admitted she had been with Jakub. She felt a spasm of guilt squeeze her midsection. Her answer came from guilt, fear, and hope.

"I'm in." She said it so faintly he almost didn't hear her.

"You're in?" he questioned.

"I'm in," she said with more conviction. "But, you need to know what I've done."

"I don't care. You just told me all I need to know." He wrapped his open palms around her and hugged her tight.

They exchanged one lengthier kiss. Their hands found each other. Daniel clasped her hand tightly.

"Let's go see our son."

33

"To take sorrow and use it as a crutch
And have all you need and never know it as such
To want the warmth of fire and get the burn of its touch
I think about you way too much."
– Mieka Pauley

With the exception of a small circle of hair loss, Phoenix recovered nicely from the radiosurgery. Macy expertly parted his hair so it was not obvious. Daniel's firm gave him a leave of absence right after the surgery and he spent every moment possible with Macy and Phoenix the first week of recovery.

Macy enjoyed having Daniel at home. Life was certainly easier to manage with the new Daniel around. He was present, helpful, and thoughtful. They established a new routine sharing duties and chores. Phoenix was elated that his father was spending nights at home again. After a follow-up appointment with Dr. Stapleton, Phoenix was cleared to resume normal activities.

Although they were not intimate, Macy feared she and Daniel were moving too fast. Some nights, she saw Jakub in her dreams, she heard his voice in her meditations, she felt his touch when she couldn't sleep. She knew she needed to be honest with Daniel about Jakub. The untold truth between them was growing more uncomfortable for her by the moment.

Macy and Daniel went to see Dr. Smithson. They sat on the plush green couch in her corner office. Natural light filled the room. Dr. Smithson sat across from Daniel and Macy with her laptop on her legs. She rarely broke eye contact with them as she rapidly typed their conversation. She tipped her head back, glancing through her red-framed bifocals then up over the rim. Macy thought Dr. Smithson would have made a great court reporter.

Dr. Smithson smiled easily when appropriate and raised her eyebrows when fitting to do so. Macy thought she made as many expressions as Mr. Bean from the hospital. But she didn't utter a word until they were finished explaining what had happened all these months. They discussed the anguish of going through Phoenix's brain tumor diagnosis and surgery. They expressed a desire to better themselves and make their marriage work. They each took responsibility for the demise of their relationship. Daniel still maintained he didn't have sex with the escorts. He expressed a desire to work one-on-one with Dr. Smithson sorting through his childhood traumas. Both he and Macy came to recognize how they had taken each other for granted. The question remained for Macy if too much had happened for them to gain confidence in each other. And of course, she wondered how Daniel would take the news about Jakub. When Dr. Smithson finally spoke, she asked very blunt, straightforward questions.

"Did you have sexual relationships with other people during your separation?"

"Yes."

Dr. Smithson clicked quickly on her keyboard.

"Would you consider those relationships to be emotional in nature, mostly sexual, or both?"

Daniel answered quickly, "Sex with Jesse was just sex for me. I never wanted anything more with her. I had emotional relationships with a number of escorts. I felt compelled to tell them horrible things about my past. I knew they wouldn't judge me because escorts usually have shitty backgrounds too. Macy's parents were awesome; I just didn't see how she could relate. So to answer your question, one of the escorts held me while I cried like a baby over my mom. She coddled me and stroked my hair. So, it was more emotional."

Dr. Smithson typed rapidly and looked up at Macy, whose face was beginning to burn.

"Macy, what about you? Would you classify your experience as emotional or sexual?"

Macy was jittery and anxious. She fought her feelings for Jakub constantly. She was plagued with fragments of conversations impaling her mind like a vortex of debris. She felt the rush of emotions when she recalled their lovemaking. That thought temporarily seized her breath. She finally answered, "Both," and then she laughed inappropriately out of nervousness. Daniel cut his eyes sideways at her but did not make eye contact.

Dr. Smithson set her laptop on a side table and leaned forward. She swept her curly flyaways behind her ear and removed her glasses. "I can see that you two have been through more than what most couples deal with. It's understandable that things broke down when you didn't have the tools to fix them. I think it's fair to say you each sought comfort in different ways. You have both expressed a desire to work things out.

"So, here's the deal, folks," she went on. "In order for me to be of service to you, we have to agree that we are going to get everything out on the table. It has been my experience that it's better to disclose everything now than to allow it to seep out in six months. In fact, I'd go as far to say that if you don't get it out now, you need to come to peace with keeping it in for the rest of your life."

Daniel interrupted, "I swear, I never had sex with the escorts. Just Jesse."

Dr. Smithson pressed, "I'm speaking to both of you."

Macy felt like Dr. Smithson was only speaking to her at that moment—as if she was psychologist and a psychic.

"It might be difficult to disclose things right now, and then add a strange old lady in front of you forcing the details out and, well…it's uncomfortable. But I would rather you be uncomfortable now than have to go through this again in six months or a year. So, let's agree this is a safe place to expose things. We are going to listen to each other with as little judgment as possible because we all have the same goal here. We all want your marriage to survive and eventually thrive. Right?"

Macy couldn't help but to wonder how many times Dr. Smithson had given that speech—but she found it to be effective, because she was more relaxed now. She thought about keeping it a secret that she had slept with Jakub and what that lie would do to them. So, Macy opened her mouth and didn't stop talking for twenty minutes. She told them about Jakub the yoga instructor, Jakub the mentor, Jakub the lover, Jakub the twin flame. Although Daniel squirmed and shifted in his seat to the point he was flustered, he didn't interrupt. She admitted that she had developed real feelings for him. In the end, she categorized her relationship as both emotional and sexual, but she spared Daniel the details that would only cause bruising to his ego. When she finished the eruption of admissions, she felt a slow decrease in the tempo of her heart rate.

Dr. Smithson allowed the silence to linger as she finished drafting Macy's narrative. Macy looked at Daniel from the side of her eyes. He was still staring at her.

"Daniel, I'm going to ask you a couple questions. I want you to think about the end result you want to achieve here. I want you to answer honestly. This is very important because it affects whether or not I can help you."

Daniel wanted to say many things. He was pissed.

"Daniel, I need you to focus on my question and answer in a complete sentence. Do you understand?"

"Yes," Daniel answered. He focused his brows at the doctor and took a breath.

Dr. Smithson continued, "Does this information Macy just told you change your decision to reconcile your marriage?"

After what felt like an hour to Macy, he finally answered, "No. I still want to reconcile my marriage with Macy."

Macy didn't realize it, but she was holding her breath while waiting on his answer.

"Okay. My next question to you is just as important. I want you to give a lot of consideration to this before answering. Please answer in a complete sentence. Do you understand?"

"Yes," he answered.

"Can you agree to never bring up, speak of, or allude to Mr. Pulaski in conversation with Macy again?"

After a still lull, he answered, "Yes. I agree to never speak of Jakub Pulaski again." He looked at Macy with tears in his eyes. Macy took the exchange to her solar plexus. She felt a space open up in her heart and a new hope that this could actually work.

Dr. Smithson shifted her body to Macy. "Macy, just because Daniel considered his liaison with Jesse to be only sexual in nature does not mean it is any less toxic to your relationship. The fact that he was hiring escorts for conversational company means there's some emotional work we need to do. So, I want you to thoughtfully answer my question in a complete sentence. Do you understand?"

"Yes ma'am," Macy answered and then felt ridiculous for adding the "ma'am."

"No matter what arguments you get into in the future, can you agree to never speak of his sexual escapade or the female escorts again?"

Macy nodded. "Yes, I agree to never bring up the sexual escapades and escorts again."

"Very good. I believe I can help you achieve your goals. So you two have been back together for…what, a few weeks? Correct?"

"That's right," answered Daniel, and Macy agreed.

"Have you engaged in sexual intercourse?" Dr. Smithson probed.

"No. We have not had sex," Macy answered.

"Good, let's keep it that way for a couple of months. We have some sorting to do, but unfortunately I'm out of time.

The most important thing has been established. We've agreed on some ground rules. Now, my receptionist will see to it that you get a regular appointment. I will see you both next week and we will take it from here. Sound good?"

They both agreed and shook her hand, thanking her for fitting them in.

When they walked out of Dr. Smithson's office, they agreed they had made significant strides. That week was the best they had together in a long time. Daniel returned to his normal work schedule and Macy to hers, though she thought of Jakub frequently. He was thousands of miles away, but the sorrow was massively thick. She grieved for him. She woke some mornings with a single thought: *Sometimes truly loving someone is accepting their decisions even when it isn't what you want.*

Dr. Smithson warned Macy that she may feel every emotion that goes with that bereavement—and she did. She prayed for Jakub's happiness and felt horrible for bringing him back into her life. She even prayed to a God she didn't believe in for help in surrendering her love for him.

Daniel and Macy learned to communicate in new ways. They enjoyed playing with Phoenix and cooking dinner together. Macy took charge of creating a weekly menu and Daniel shopped for the ingredients. He taught Macy how to read his financial graphs and pie charts of expenses. She asked him questions about basketball, video games he enjoyed, and other topics that interested him. Macy made an effort to be more organized but she also continued to let her hair go back to dreadlocks. They both respected and even admired each other for their differences again. In fact, Macy found those differences to be the very thing that allowed her to be most authentic now. Phoenix was flourishing. Their laughs were legitimate and heartfelt. Macy appreciated that Daniel had come so far in his ability to relinquish control. He was proving himself to be trustworthy. He shared things about his mother's mental health—how, when Daniel was fourteen, she attempted suicide and he found her passed out, naked in a bloody bathtub with pills surrounding her. He suspected she was bipolar. He shared his fear of sharing the same fate. He had decided to stop drinking alcohol on his own.

The following week in counseling, they picked up where they left off. But it seemed they were past the most difficult part. The air around them was lighter. Dr. Smithson gave them homework and tools for communicating more effectively so they didn't run into a similar situation down the road. She taught them how to mindfully listen. She requested they read books on mindful behavior. Dr. Smithson was pleased with their progress but warned them not to get too carried away with any other major life decision and encouraged abstinence for the time being. Whenever Macy and Daniel ran into a situation that they feared would cause them turbulence, they agreed to table that discussion for a time when Dr. Smithson could mediate.

A couple of weeks later, Macy had to miss the appointment with Dr. Smithson because she had a stomach bug. From the moment she got up that morning until she went to sleep, she vomited. All the household duties fell on Daniel but he was thoughtful about keeping Phoenix away from Macy. Neither of them wanted Phoenix to catch her virus this soon after his turmoil. Daniel made Macy's favorite chicken soup but the smell seemed overly pungent to Macy, causing her to gag and heave again. This went on for several days. Daniel was concerned that she couldn't keep food down and insisted on taking her to the doctor. Reluctantly she agreed. She was becoming concerned about how much rest she needed and secretly wondered if she might have a brain tumor also.

The next day, Daniel helped her into the waiting room. He sat her on the exam table, made sure she was stable, and turned to leave.

"Daniel, please stay," she asked. If she was going to get diagnosed with a brain tumor, she wanted him there.

The nurse came in and measured Macy's blood pressure, temperature, pulse and asked the standard questions.

"How long have you been sick?"

"What symptoms have you had?"

"Do you have any allergies?"

"What's the first day of your last period?"

That question stumped Macy. Life had been a whirlwind.

"Is there any chance you could be pregnant?" the nurse asked.

Silence. Macy couldn't be sure.

"Ma'am. Is it possible that you could be pregnant?" the nurse exhaled with a snicker. She pointed her finger at the couple. "Lots of accidents result in little heartbeats, you know. I should not have to tell you how to use protection." She laughed at her own joke as she hoisted Macy up.

"Come on, sweetie, I'm going to need you to urinate in this cup. Write your first and last name on it and the last four digits of your social security number." She chuckled. She sat Macy on the toilet. "Let me know if you need help."

Macy leaned against the counter for balance and held the cup under her stream of urine. Memories of the night with Jakub flashed through her mind. She saw the top of Jakub's head at the edge of the bed coaxing the tampon out of her vagina. She had not had a period since they made love.

She slid the specimen through the metal door just over the commode. Hers was the only sample in there. She and Daniel had not had sex since before they separated.

Macy lurched over the seat and upchucked in the wastebasket. She didn't want to come out of the bathroom. She sat for a long time.

Eventually Macy gathered her balance and stumbled her way back to the exam room. She opened the door. Daniel didn't look at her face. After a moment he asked, "You didn't use a condom, did you?"

She was hesitant but answered honestly. "No."

Daniel restrained himself from saying anything else that would break the promise he made to never speak of this man again.

Before either of them had a chance to think much more, the nurse bustled into the room. "Looks like you don't have a virus, missy. You're pregnant! Congratulations, you two!"

They rode home in silence. Daniel wiped his face forcefully, as if he wanted to remove this day from existence. Stunned, Macy stared out the passenger window.

When they got home, instead of helping Macy out of the car, Daniel went into their bedroom and shut the door. Macy feebly got to the kitchen table and contemplated how this could have happened. She was on her period. She knew it was possible to conceive, but very unlikely...she thought. She wondered what Daniel was thinking. She wondered if he had used a condom with Jesse. She thought about calling Dr. Smithson for an emergency therapy session.

Macy couldn't deny a small part of her heart was happy. She hated herself for feeling joy, but she did. She had wanted to have another child so badly. It was Jakub's DNA growing inside of her this time. Still, to know a life was inside of her was magic. She grew stronger and began pacing the floors. A quiet resolve grew in the deepest part of her. Macy looked at herself in the mirror positioned near the kitchen.

"How can you feel happy about this?" she asked herself. "You are really fucked up in the head." She placed her palm under her belly button and allowed her fingers to cup her stomach. She tenderly feathered her stomach back and forth much like the way Oona had feathered her arm in the hospital with Phoenix. Macy marveled at how strong the maternal instinct could be.

Hours had gone by without a word from Daniel. Things had been so good between them again. A calm, steady, slow appreciation and admiration was growing. They were once again a good balance to one another. They were finding their rhythm again. Phoenix was so happy to have his parents together again. Now, she was amazed at the depth of her confusion and despair.

Just before Phoenix was to arrive home, Macy summoned the courage to knock on the bedroom door.

"Daniel?" she whispered softly.

He opened the door and stood with his fingers still wrapped around the handle. "You have to have an abortion," he said flatly.

"*Daniel!* You can't ask me to do that. You know I can't do that. After everything we went through with Phoenix? We know what a fetus looks like. There's no way I could harm a baby." She paused. "Please don't ask me to do that."

Daniel was quiet for a long time. Meekly he asked, "Are you going to leave me? Are you going to leave Phoenix? Are you going to leave us and start a family with him?" His voice was weak. It was the most vulnerable she had ever seen Daniel. She could see the insecurity in his eyes.

"What? No!" She pushed the door open. She wrapped her arms around him. "Daniel, you chose me and I chose you. It's done."

He collapsed in tears. "I can't believe this is happening to us," he admitted. "We just got our shit straight and we get another curveball."

In all the years they had known each other, Macy had never seen him so dismayed. He was sobbing.

"Maybe I should call and request a session with Dr. Smithson," she said. "Maybe she could help us make sense of this."

"No. Not yet."

"Why not?" Macy asked.

"Because...I don't know. I don't know! UGH! I don't know! Okay?!" He fell silent for a moment. "I just think we need to think of our options, Macy."

"What options do we have?"

"Adoption."

That night, Macy dreamed that Dr. Smithson was counseling her.

"You see—you were infatuated with Mr. Pulaski. Intense feelings like this never last. Passion always subsides. You experienced a release of chemicals in your brain with Mr. Pulaski. These are the same chemicals released in people that have addictions to drugs or alcohol. They weren't real feelings. Nothing that will last more than a few months. Let it go."

Then her Sunday School teacher walked into Dr. Smithson's office. "It's the devil. He's the devil. Satan made you do it."

Macy woke up drenched.

34

"I bite my tongue 'cause all I do is stutter
Tell me things you wouldn't tell your mother
I take your little hand 'cause I'd really love to dance
With you, across the kitchen floor."
– Lonely Neighbor

Daniel and Macy agreed not to tell anyone about the pregnancy right away—not even Dr. Smithson. They agreed to consider adoption. After Daniel went to work each day, Macy climbed back into bed and lay in the fetal position. For hours, she caressed her belly and sang to her unborn child. She sensed it was a boy. She spoke out loud to him. She cried and explained why she was going to give him up.

During the first trimester of her pregnancy, her dreams were vivid with imagery. Often the dreams began with two thick roots deep inside the earth's surface, intertwining and emerging as the stalk of a single sunflower sharing the same blueprint. She frequently woke up in the early hours of the morning and cried softly into her pillow. She telepathically begged for Jakub's forgiveness.

Daniel slept quietly beside her. On the weekends, Daniel was able to see the effects of the morning sickness. Macy was never sick when she was pregnant with Phoenix. This pregnancy produced spells of violent retching. Macy would stubbornly try to cook dinner and be as normal as possible but she had an aversion to most food and smells.

Daniel insisted Macy put her swollen feet up. He would bring her a cold cloth for her forehead and stack her feet on a mountain of pillows. He whisked hair out of her face when she was sick and kept a cup of ginger tea by her side to settle her stomach. Macy was grateful for his earnest gestures of kindness. The way he took care of her, one would mistake this baby to be his own.

Toward the middle of her second trimester, Macy was beginning to look pregnant. She had slowly withdrawn from society and quit her job. The first one to notice Macy's protruding tummy was Phoenix. Daniel delicately explained to Phoenix that Mommy had a sick baby in her belly and that the baby would go straight to Heaven. Phoenix seemed to accept this information without many questions, but Macy found drawings in his school bag. One portrait was of their family. Each person had been labeled. Macy's stick figure included a bump on her stomach with an arrow pointing to "my baby brother or sister going to Heaven." She knew he was processing this information in his own way and felt terrible for lying to him.

In the middle of her second trimester, Macy still had not gone to any prenatal doctor exams. She knew the baby was healthy. She could feel it moving and growing. She believed more than ever it was a boy.

At the beginning of her third trimester, Macy was more pregnant than she had ever been with Phoenix. During her meditations, Macy held visions of what Jakub's baby would look like mixed with her genes. She wondered if he would favor her or Jakub. She thought of his genetics, his jawline, his teeth, his eye color. She thought of his little brother, Niko, who died drinking bleach. She pondered what Jakub's parents were like and if their grandson would possess characteristics of their ancestry. She wondered if he would be drawn to Central European history in school. She replayed her conversation with Jakub from the inn and remembered him saying he didn't have any allergies. She wondered if her child would be angry or hurt that he was given away. She fantasized about telling Jakub she was pregnant. Sometimes she allowed herself to pretend Phoenix was a big brother. The larger she grew, the closer she felt to her son and the deeper the torment she experienced.

She felt the first flutter of her baby move in the early hours after a particularly remarkable dream. Jakub was standing across from her. At first he was a mirror image of her. But the image morphed into a clear vision of Jakub. There was a blazing blue ball of light under his sternum. Macy was directly in front of him, a brilliant red ball of light in the middle of her breastbone. Their hands were attached, grasping each other, but their heads and torsos were leaning away from each other. Cyclones and twisters lashed around them. Macy gripped tightly to Jakub's hand as the wind snapped around them.

"Don't let go!" Jakub yelled over the windstorm. "Just hold on."

The storm grew more violent. Jakub used every fiber of his muscle to draw Macy into his chest.

"I'm trying!" she yelled over the roaring wind.

For a flash, the luminous balls connected. In the midst of the blustering gale, a radiant shimmering spectrum shot up between them. Jakub could see Macy through the beam of light. His clutch was strong. His expression had transformed to tranquility. He smiled harmoniously at Macy. She exhaled with relief. Butterflies began to materialize out of the light. She and Jakub looked up in wonder. A blissful feeling unfolded, wrapping around them, protecting them from the wind. Then Macy woke up to the quickening of her baby inside her womb. The baby's movement felt like the wings of a butterfly.

When Oona finally recognized Macy was pregnant and not just gaining weight, she was elated. "Oh my goodness! I can't believe you didn't tell me! Oh, but I understand. When can I tell the girls at bridge?" She went on about how she wished Carl could have lived to love another grandchild.

Oona threw her arms around Daniel. "I just knew you two would work this out. I just knew it! I'm so happy I get to be a grandmother again." She pinched Daniel's cheek and hugged him again. She danced around them in cheer, flailing her arms.

Daniel was twisting inside. He wanted to celebrate her reaction as if it was reality. He wanted to be the father of this successful pregnancy. Searing pain shot through him, seeing Oona so enthused.

"Does Phoenix know he's going to be a big brother?" Oona asked.

Daniel and Macy reticently exchanged looks. When Oona finally detected his reserve, she looked to Macy for clarity. Daniel promptly excused himself from the room.

And so it began. Macy laid down the first layer of deception. She hated lying to her mother. The story Macy and Daniel had fabricated would cause her mother a multitude of heartache. Macy spit the erroneous story out so fast it was like pulling off a Band-Aid.

Predictably, Oona took the news in agony. She sat in her own grief and despair then offered Macy compassion and sympathy. Macy felt like a fraud accepting her mother's warmth and tenderness. She wanted to tell her the truth—this baby wasn't going to die, that it was perfect, healthy, and conceived in a union of soul-quaking love. She wanted to share the entire truth with her mom—that she was choosing Daniel and Phoenix. But she denied herself the luxury of having the relief that sweet honesty would offer her. She wanted to accept her mother's consoling hugs. The atrocity of lying to Oona made Macy feel beyond cruel. She felt cold-blooded.

Over the next month, Macy pushed Oona away. Oona kept making attempts to see her daughter, but Macy had an excuse every time. Anything to keep from discussing the lies. Oona offered to tell neighbors and friends about the defected baby Macy was carrying to save Macy the pain of retelling the horror. Macy wished her mother could be self-centered and unconcerned for Macy. But Oona loved her daughter devoutly.

Daniel knew lying to Oona was killing Macy. He tried to think of ways to make the situation better. One morning he heard Macy crying in the bathroom. He knocked.

"Macy, you don't have to hide your emotions from me. I'm a part of this too," he said softly through the door.

He went back down on their bed and noticed a CD on Macy's bedside table. It was music from their wedding. He slipped it into his laptop and pressed play. "When a Man Loves A Woman" came through the speakers.

Macy opened the door and looked confused at the music. Daniel stood and held his hand out to her. Her eyes were puffy, her skin was blotchy, and her belly was protruded. Daniel had never seen her more beautiful. He pulled her close and gently placed his hand under her armpits, lifting her bare feet on top of his. He sang every word in her ear as he swayed back and forth. He kissed her tears as they fell and held her tight.

Macy's dreams intensified. She dreamed of a time when she was young and carefree. She was driving a convertible down the road with her elbow propped up on the door. The air was the perfect temperature. One of Macy's favorite songs was on the radio. She extended her arm out the window, and it caught the wind. She spread her fingers wide and felt the breeze push through each digit. She flexed her wrist so that it was snaking the breeze. The wind tousled her hair. She felt free—then sadness seeped in and woke her.

Macy and Daniel found an adoption agency and filtered through all the information. Confidentiality was of the utmost importance. Two weeks before the baby was due, arrangements were made. The day Macy's water broke, Daniel drove her to the small country hospital in Duplin County.

The attending physician appeared to be in his mid twenties. He explained that the baby's head was crowning. There wasn't time for Macy to receive an epidural. She would have to deliver vaginally.

Daniel protested on Macy's behalf. He didn't think it would be safe for her to deliver vaginally after her C-section. Macy was not prepared for this. She had not planned on seeing her baby but now it was too late. The baby was coming.

Daniel left the room to call the rep from the adoption agency, and when he returned, Macy was pushing. He held her head and gently encouraged her. "It's almost out. I can see its head. Keep pushing."

Macy looked at Daniel and for a moment wished it was his child she was delivering. He had been amazing through this pregnancy. He had fallen in love with her even more because she agreed to give up Jakub's baby. He knew she loved the child and that it would tear her apart to place it up for adoption. To him, it meant she desperately wanted to work things out for their family.

The agency worker arrived. The nurse whispered to the doctor that this was an adoption case. The doctor seemed surprised as he eyed the couple.

Macy gave one final push and her son took his first breath.

The doctor lifted the baby up so Macy could see. "You've got a perfect baby boy here."

Her instinct was correct—it was a boy. Macy glowed at the sight of him. The baby let out a powerful wail and Macy laughed through her tears. Macy thought about how easy the labor was compared to what she experienced with Phoenix.

A nurse cleaned the child and brought him to Macy. "Here's your son. He's ready to eat."

Macy looked at Daniel for approval. "Just for the colostrum? Please, Daniel. Just one feeding."

The adrenaline was overwhelming to Daniel despite the baby not being his biological son. This had been the birth experience they always pictured for Phoenix.

"Daniel, please?" Macy pressed.

Everyone blinked, waiting for Daniel's approval. Daniel cautiously nodded. He watched Macy nurse Jakub's son.

"I almost think I could love him like my own, Macy," Daniel said hopefully.

After a long silence, Macy spoke. "I believe you could love him today, Daniel. But what about when he's five or ten and he resembles another man?"

Daniel was quiet for a long time. "I don't know."

Daniel needed to think clearly. The delicate situation had clouded his judgment. He walked around the perimeter of the building, pacing like an expectant father. He ran his fingers through his hair and looked up at the sky. It had become a beautiful day—as if everything was perfect in the world.

He sat on a lonely bench shaded by an evergreen. He watched people enter and exit the hospital doors and wondered why they were here. Doubting any of them could relate to his experience, he felt isolated from the world. He had not spoken to his sisters or his parents in a long time; they had no idea what was going on.

He sat doubting this whole plan. It was crazy to think this would work but he still hoped. The only thing he knew for sure is that he loved Macy with all of his heart. He believed they could move past this.

On the way back to Macy's delivery room, he stopped at the gift shop. There was only one bouquet of flowers in the little refrigerator. The shop owner smiled.

"They're a little wilted; I'll give them to you half off." She winked and handed him the change.

The agency worker gave Macy privacy while she nursed her son for the first and last time. In her moments alone with the child, she lifted him up eye level to her. She examined his perfection. His eyelashes were long and dark; his nose was smashed and wide like Jakub's.

"You are a spitting image of your father but you've got my eyes, I see." She stared at him in awe, captured in a bubble of time for just the two of them. She drew him to her nose and inhaled his familiar scent. He, too, smelled like home.

"I have known you for moments but I have loved you for lifetimes. I hope someday you'll forgive me. I wish I had done things differently. Please always know you are an angel made from love. You were meant to be here."

Macy cried and whispered softly with her lips touching his face. "I don't know if I'm doing the right thing. I wish I had a sign." She pulled him away and admired his resemblance to Jakub.

Daniel came in and paused briefly at the sight of Macy speaking to her son. He had never seen her look at anyone more adoringly than they way she was smiling down at her new child.

Macy looked up and saw Daniel through the crack of the door. Daniel held the floral arrangement up for Macy to see. She couldn't hide her astonishment. The smile vanished from her face. She eyeballed the profusion of sunflowers as if there was an esoteric inscription scrolling across the frond.

Daniel went about the business of putting the bouquet of sunflowers in a plastic vase. Macy followed him with her gaze. She wondered if her body would always have this physiological response to the sight of sunflowers.

The agency rep came back in.

"Mrs. Westcott? Remember, you'll have seven days to change your mind," she said reassuringly—as if that was enough time to know they were doing the right thing. "You can be as anonymous or as involved as you want to be with regard to the adoptive parents. You get to call all the shots."

Macy asked the worker to take her picture with her son. Macy's eyes were brimming with tears as the flash went off. The intensity of her emotional pain translated in a howling desolate cry. She would have preferred death in that moment over her excruciating agony.

Macy lifted her son and pressed her lips repeatedly all over his face, inhaling his scent between each one. She tried to focus her eyes through her tears. She blinked her vision clear and willed herself to take a snapshot of his face with her mind's eye. She smelled him again. He smelled like her tapestry, like Jakub and like returning home. She whispered promises into his ear. The sentences came quick with modulation. She kissed him on his mouth and smelled his head for a long inhale.

"Mrs. Westcott, this is never easy. I have a lovely couple who is waiting for a phone call to adopt your son. What would you like me to say?" the agency worker asked.

Daniel looked ardently for Macy's response.

"Tell them…tell them…."

Macy hiccupped through her sobs.

She passed her son to the agency worker.

"Please tell them his name is Niko."

The End

Acknowledgements

DeLisa Alexander, my amazing friend and sister – Your strength and determination is awe-inspiring. You are a talented leader, a brilliant woman, a compassionate sister, and so much more. Life has thrown you many lemons, to which you say, "Let's have some fucking lemonade."

Baird and Marlene – There are many types of love. It is rare to see them all exhibited by two people the way you have. Thank you for the example of a truly beautiful relationship.

John Kilpatrick – If I cracked open your sternum, there's a good possibility I might strike gold. How fortunate for me to be your baby sister. Sister Hazel and The Eagles. That is all.

Mom and Dad – For accepting my decisions, though you don't always understand why. You are the salt of the Earth. If the world had more parents like you, it would be a better place in which to live. Your generosity with love, touch, time, and kindness makes me a better person and mother. Your moral compass yet forgiving nature has helped me to embrace my numerous flaws. I'm glad I chose you and you chose me back. Let's rendezvous again next lifetime.

Kade Rivers – In your genes, you received the best of your father and the best of me. Your intuitive gifts, compassion, empathy, and gentle nature make you an incredible young man. I'm honored beyond measure for the gift of being your momma. Remember this: Anyone who gets to be in your life is blessed. Period.

For Brody's birth mother – Thank you for your selfless choice to place your son for adoption. You have enriched my life in remarkable ways. I am grateful for you every single day.

Brody Hawke – You are a badass in training. You are the tether that keeps me present. You brought laughter to my heart when I thought there would be no more.

Alisa Smithson – For recognizing the tight bud would eventually have to burst or bloom. For what may seem as chaos to some, you saw as an emergence of authenticity. As I stood at the edge of the cliff, it was your voice that said, "Spread your wings first, then jump." Thank you for your constant faith in me.

Chrissy Clark-Sopina – Every now and then you meet someone who is able to connect through unspoken words, like a supernatural phenomenon. It's been over twenty-five years. As I wrote this sentence, you called. ;)

Julie Billado – Your thoughtfulness is inspiring and my respect for you is untouchable. Thank you for continuing to remind me that it's okay to be a butterfly.

Alison Ferreira, my Yoda – Your friendship has encouraged me to embrace the uncertainty and believe in miracles. I am certain we have walked beside each other as warriors over many lifetimes. Thank you for always having my back.

Ashley Hughes – Over thirty years you have had my admiration for being uniquely you. I love that you follow your heart and dreams despite the opinions of the peanut gallery. When you keep yourself in the flow, all is well. Remind me of this later.

Hassina and my yogini sisterhood – Sometimes the universe conspires to thread lives together for a purpose we do not fully comprehend. Such was the case with our YTT. You made a difficult time easier without even knowing the role you were playing. I'm forever grateful to know each of you.

Lynn – For being the first to cry for Macy and encouraging me to continue writing.

Dawn – Avoid egg rolls when I'm not there to do the Heimlich. Your honest feedback made Macy a better character.

For Daria – When I saw your art, I knew it was Macy. Thank you for letting me tweak her. It was a pleasure to work with so much talent.

Kristen – I'm especially grateful for the fact you didn't like Macy. You helped me weigh the options of maintaining my authenticity versus "cleaning up" some of her flaws for the comfort of the reader. It helped me articulate my need to develop rich characters who are messy and flawed – just like real people. Thank you for your valuable edits. You have found your calling.

For Tara Wilder – Thank you for sitting with me on my front porch to discussing the plot ad nauseam. Your eagle eye, feedback and time is worth more than I can adequately express.

Karee, Kate, Robin – Three women who do motherhood exceedingly well. I believe they chose you because no one else would have done motherhood better than you in this lifetime. Cheers to the children who make us stronger women.

For every major transformation in life that ignites a metamorphosis, there is a catalyst. That catalyst might be a person, an event, or perhaps a growing whisper deep inside the soul bubbling to the surface. The awakening may be considered simply good or bad but largely falls into a more complex category that evokes an emersion of change. Sometimes the catalyst may hold a flame to a dormant truth – a magnifying glass to what you pretended not to see. Once it is awakened and the transformation begins. For me, retrogression was not an option. Cheers to the trezire.

Made in the USA
Middletown, DE
25 June 2016